S0-EAY-511

WITHDRAWN

DATE DUE

JUL 9 1991	JUL 1 6 1998
MAR 2 0 1992	SEP 9 -
APR 2 7 1992	DEC 0 2 1998
JUN 2 4 1992	JUN 0 2
MAR 2 2 1993	MAY 0 8 2000
MAY 3 1 1993	APR _ 3 2000
AUG 1993	OCT 2 1 2005
	NOV 2 8 2006
MAR 22 1995	DEC 1 9 2006
	FEB 1 9 2007
DEC 14 1995	DEC 1 2 2007
	JAN 0 6 2021
JAN 0 5 1996	APR 0 6 2021
DEC 1 5 1996	
DEC 1 9 1996	
FEB 1 1 1998	

HIGHSMITH   # 45220

MARS

OTHER BOOKS BY JAMES A. CORRICK

Double Your Pleasure

Farm Animals

The Human Brain:
Mind and Matter

The Planet Seekers

Recent Revolutions
in Biology

Recent Revolutions
in Chemistry

MARS

JAMES A. CORRICK

Franklin Watts
New York   London   Toronto   Sydney   1991
A Venture Book

Photographs courtesy of: Lowell Observatory: p. 15; NASA: pp. 20, 29, 42 right, 45, 56, 63, 78, 84, 88; Holiday Film Corporation: p. 25 left; Photo Researchers Inc.: p. 42 left (NASA), Hansen Planetarium: p. 27; Woods Hole Oceanographic Institution: p. 67; National Science Foundation, Division of Polar Programs: p. 69; Movie Star News: p. 100; Photofest: pp. 103, 108, 110, 111.

Library of Congress Cataloging-in-Publication Data

Corrick, James A.
  Mars / by James A. Corrick.
    p.   cm. — (A Venture book)
  Includes bibliographical references and index.
  Summary: Describes the atmosphere and surface of Mars, including recent findings from NASA space probes, and surveys the history of our attempts to discover more about this planet.
  ISBN 0-531-12528-9
  1. Mars (Planet)—Juvenile literature. 2. Mars (Planet)—Exploration—Juvenile literature. [1. Mars (Planet) 2. Outer space—Exploration.] I. Title.
  QB641.C68   1991
  523.4′3—dc20   90-22083 CIP AC

To Gay,
who would also like to stand on
the summit of Olympus Mons

CONTENTS

1
FINDING OUT ABOUT MARS 11

2
THE GEOLOGY OF MARS 23

3
THE WATERS OF MARS 39

4
THE CLIMATE OF MARS 50

5
LIFE ON MARS 62

6
THE MOONS OF MARS 72

7
THE BECKONING LURE OF MARS 83

8
THE FICTIONAL MARS 96

Appendix 1
THE PHYSICAL CHARACTERISTICS
OF MARS AND EARTH 113

Appendix 2
THE ATMOSPHERE OF
MARS AND EARTH 114

Appendix 3
THE PHYSICAL CHARACTERISTICS OF
PHOBOS, DEIMOS, AND THE MOON 115

Appendix 4
MISSIONS TO MARS 116

Glossary 119

For Further Reading
and Viewing 120

Index 123

MARS

1

FINDING OUT ABOUT MARS

Mars is the fourth planet from the Sun, being the next planet out after the Earth. For most of human history, Mars was nothing more than a red dot that every twenty-six months appeared and blossomed in the night sky before once more disappearing from sight. Ancient peoples saw its sinister color as that of blood and took its appearance as an omen of approaching war or famine. Mars's various names reflect this bloody reputation. The ancient Babylonians called it *Nergal*, god of both war and the dead; the Persians labeled it *Pahlavani Siphir*, the celestial warrior; and the Greeks knew it as *Ares*, god of battle. Even our current name for the planet follows this tradition, since Mars was the Roman god of war. War-related words such as *martial*, meaning warlike, come from the same Latin root.

EARLY DISCOVERIES

The invention of the telescope in the early 1600s turned Mars into a world. In 1659 the Dutch mathe-

11

matician and astronomer Christian Huygens drew the first maps showing surface features on Mars. His drawings contain a white cap resting atop one Martian pole, as well as a large, wedge-shaped dark area. Other astronomers soon spotted a similar cap at Mars's other pole. At the same time, they saw several other dark areas that formed distinct patterns against the rest of Mars's red surface.

Observers of the late eighteenth century such as Sir William Herschel, discoverer of the planet Uranus, had better telescopes. Herschel watched Mars and noticed that each Martian polar cap grew and shrank depending on the time of year. Herschel naturally assumed that the polar caps were ice and were similar to the caps covering the Earth's North and South Poles, which partially melt in the spring and summer and refreeze in fall and winter. By timing the appearance and disappearance of the dark areas, he found that a Martian day was about thirty minutes longer than a terrestrial one. Herschel was also the first astronomer to claim that Mars had an atmosphere.

The dark areas remained a mystery. Mars was too far away, and early telescopes were not powerful enough to reveal much detail. Seeing that Mars had ice caps like those on Earth, early Mars watchers reasoned that Mars might also have continents and oceans. They decided that the red areas were land and the dark regions seas. These observations and conclusions led astronomers to look more and more on Mars as a second Earth. They even began thinking of the fourth planet as a possible second home for life in the solar system.

These eighteenth-century Mars observers, however, discovered that Mars was not exactly like Earth. Measuring its size, they discovered that Mars was smaller than Earth. The smaller size of Mars meant that its surface gravity was weaker than the Earth's.

Eighteenth-century astronomers realized that with its lower surface gravity Mars could not hold as thick an atmosphere as Earth. Yet, they did not think it so thin that it could not support life, and all of them assumed that the atmosphere of Mars had oxygen in it.

These early Mars watchers were also certain that the fourth planet was colder than the Earth because it was much farther away from the Sun. Calculations showed that Mars never approached the Sun closer than 128 million miles (205 million kilometers), in contrast to the Earth's orbit of 93 million miles (150 million kilometers). Astronomers determined that Mars took almost twice as long, 687 days, to orbit the Sun as did the Earth. They logically assumed that each of its four seasons—spring, summer, fall, and winter—was longer and cooler than those on Earth.

THE CANALS OF MARS

In the 1870s the Italian astronomer Giovanni Schiaparelli claimed that he saw faint lines running between the dark areas. Like most of his contemporaries, Schiaparelli believed these regions to be oceans, and he was convinced that these connecting lines were natural waterways or channels, which in Italian are called *canali*. He soon found himself, however, the father of the Martian canals. The European press, particularly English-speaking reporters, quickly corrupted the word *canali* to mean canals or artificial waterways. Canals meant not only life, but intelligent life.

Not all astronomers accepted the existence of these surface lines. Asaph Hall of the U.S. Naval Observatory, discoverer of Mars's two moons, could see no trace of these channels. Hall ridiculed the whole notion that such waterways existed on Mars.

The existence of intelligent Martians depended

entirely on the observation of some questionable lines on the surface of a distant planet. There was no other evidence, and the search for that intelligent life over the 35 million miles (56 million kilometers) separating Earth and Mars at their closest approach to each other was done mostly in the imaginations of the searchers.

The most imaginative of those looking for signs of intelligent life on Mars was the American astronomer Percival Lowell (Figure 1). Lowell became interested in astronomy while an undergraduate at Harvard, but upon graduation he turned instead to business, in which he quickly made his fortune. In 1893 he turned once more to astronomy. He was fascinated by the canals of Mars. Lowell believed that the canals were the work of an intelligent species, and he spared no pains or expense to find and provide the world with proof of his belief. He even went so far as to found his own observatory, the Lowell Observatory, outside Flagstaff, Arizona.

Lowell made what he maintained were detailed maps (Figure 2) of the Martians' canal system. He even claimed to have seen a canal being built! After supposedly spotting a canal within one of the dark areas, Lowell concluded that these areas were not bodies of water, but rather regions covered with plants. No one had been able to decide on the exact color of

Figure 1. Above: Percival Lowell at work in his observatory in Flagstaff, Arizona. Figure 2. Below: Percival Lowell made numerous drawings showing the intricate canal system that he believed covered the face of Mars and was the work of intelligent beings.

these areas, but some astronomers claimed they were green. Lowell had no doubts that these regions were colored green, the green of living plants.

Lowell's conclusion fitted another observation of the dark regions: they changed shape. To Lowell, these changes were seasonal: during the summer, the areas expanded as the plants grew; during the winter, they shrank as the plants died.

Lowell further decided that, if no open bodies of water existed on Mars, then water was very scarce, and the fourth planet must be a desert world. The various dark areas were oases of life. Lowell's Martians strove to keep themselves alive by routing the scanty Martian water supply found at each pole across immense wastelands to the Martian farmlands.

Lowell presented these ideas about the fourth planet in his 1896 book, *Mars*. His picture of the Martians' heroic battle to survive on their dry world quickly grabbed the reading public's imagination. Such ideas did not sit well with other astronomers. Lowell's defense of his Mars and his Martians was so fierce that he earned the anger and contempt of many of his contemporaries—not only astronomers but also other scientists. Nor was Lowell's case helped when other astronomers failed to see his elaborate canal system.

DIFFICULT OBSERVATIONS

Why did some nineteenth-century astronomers see these surface lines while others didn't? One major problem in observing Mars was its distance from Earth. Even at its closest approach, the fourth planet was still 35 million miles (56 million kilometers) from earthbound astronomers, 145 times farther than the Moon. The small size of the fourth planet was another obstacle to detailed observation. Mars was, therefore, so far away and so small that even the most powerful turn-of-the-century telescopes could produce no more than a relatively small image of the planet. Only the largest Martian features were clearly visible.

Photography in the nineteenth century was not developed enough to produce detailed pictures with telescopes, so practically all pictures of Mars were drawings made by astronomers. Each astronomer sat with an eye pressed to the telescope's eyepiece, often in a freezing observatory, and drew what he saw or thought he saw. Because the reflected light from the planet was twisted and shaken by its passage through the turbulent, thick atmosphere of Earth, the observer often had to wait hours, sometimes the entire night, for a view of Mars sufficiently clear to reveal more than a few details. Clear viewing rarely lasted more than a few minutes, and the astronomer was forced to sketch what he saw as rapidly as possible.

Such conditions were far from ideal for checking on the reality of the canals of Mars. Even canal supporters admitted that the lines were faint and difficult to see. The very faintness of the canals and the difficulty of viewing Mars led the critics to call the canals optical illusions.

A British scientist, E. Walter Maunder, set out in 1913 to prove that the canals were an optical illusion. Maunder believed that the surface of Mars was covered with a larger number of small features. He claimed that the human eye, barely able to see such features over the long distance separating Mars and Earth, would blend them together to form the continuous lines of the canals.

Maunder's experiment had a group of thirteen-year-old boys with good eyesight but no knowledge of, or interest in, Mars sit facing a sketch of the fourth planet, within which were little dots and small, irregular shapes. Maunder told the boys to draw what they saw. The nearest boys drew in the dots and other shapes, since they could clearly see all the markings, while those farthest away, who could see only the general outline of the drawing, drew none of those shapes. The boys in the middle, however, sketched lines running across Mars. These boys were at the right distance for their eyes to be fooled into seeing all the marks as lines. Canal supporters dismissed Maunder's experiment and conclusions as nonsense.

A COLD, LIFELESS WORLD

In the twentieth century, worthwhile planetary photographs were finally taken through telescopes. None showed the slightest trace of canals or channels on Mars. This lack of photographic evidence did not diminish the enthusiasm of the canal supporters, and they still reported canal sightings. The canal spotters pointed out that even the clearest photographs of Mars were blurrier than what could be seen with the naked eye, showing little more than the grossest of details—the ice caps and the dark and red areas.

During the first half of the twentieth century, astronomers became increasingly interested in studying stars and galaxies, and they spent less time observing any of the planets, including Mars. Yet some observations of Mars continued. Thermal measurement of Martian surface temperatures showed that Mars was indeed very cold. Most of the time the surface temperature was tens of degrees below the freezing point of water.

Telescopic studies of the dark regions showed that they were not green but red. Lowell's "farmlands" were actually as red as the surrounding areas, but dust blowing across these areas cut down on the amount of light reflected back into space, making them appear darker than the surrounding regions. It was also this blowing dust that caused the expansion and contraction of these dark areas. Mars had no large spreads of vegetation. The canals of Mars then had nothing to irrigate. Added to the lack of photographic evidence, this new finding was one more argument against the canals' existence.

THE ANCIENT FACE OF MARS

The deathblow to the canals came on July 14, 1965, when the American spacecraft *Mariner 4* flew to within 16,000 miles (10,000 kilometers) of the Martian surface. With twenty-two pictures of the planet's southern hemisphere, the spacecraft destroyed forever the notion of Martian canals. The canals of Mars were an optical illusion. The eyes of canal observers seeing small surface objects just on the edge of visibility had merged them into the continuous lines of the Martian canals, just what the British scientist Maunder had suspected.

The Mars that the probe revealed was an arid landscape, devoid of any remarkable features save the thousands of ancient asteroid and meteorite craters dotting the surface (Figure 3). Not a single canal was seen then or afterward in any survey of the Martian surface by planetary probes.

In the summer of 1969, NASA's *Mariners 6* and 7 orbited Mars. They surveyed the same southern hemisphere, as well as the equatorial region, and sent back pictures of more craters. The most disappointing news was the probes' failure to find water, although they did find evidence of possible water erosion. The South Polar cap was frozen carbon dioxide and appeared to have no water in it at all. Carbon dioxide is the gas that our lungs exhale. Frozen carbon dioxide is dry ice.

The southern hemisphere that *Mariners 4, 6,* and 7 photographed was a flat plain full of old craters (Figure 3). Although some of the craters were recent, most

19

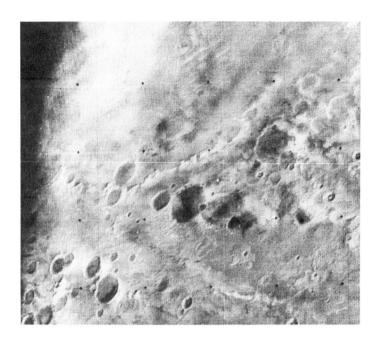

Figure 3. Mars's southern crater-pocked terrain,
as photographed by Mariner 7 in 1969.

were eroded and dust-filled. The largest was the Hellas Basin, almost 1,000 miles (1,600 kilometers)
across and 2.5 miles (4 kilometers) deep. Nineteenth-
century astronomers had thought it was a large desert
oasis.

This crater-pocked terrain was old and appeared
to have changed little in the last 3 or 4 billion years.
Since strikes by asteroids are rare, happening once
every 100 million years or so, any planetary surface
with large numbers of big craters must be ancient. On
Earth, an active geology erased our world's ancient
craters. Where wind and rain didn't erode away the
rims and floors, lava covered them, oceans drowned
them, mountains buried them, and continents slid

over them. The Martian surface the Mariner space-craft photographed appeared to have experienced none of these geologic events—at least not in billions of years.

GETTING A BETTER LOOK

The Mars shown in the photographs transmitted by *Mariners 4, 6,* and 7 was virtually as dead as the Moon it resembled. It was not a dying world. It was a dead world, and it had died billions of years ago. Space-age technology had finally allowed scientists to see Mars close up, but it had also destroyed the myth of the second Earth. Or had it?

The three Mariner spacecraft had photographed only 20 percent of the planet's surface. Large portions of Mars still remained unknown, although many astronomers felt that these would merely repeat the pattern of the known area. Still, a new U.S. probe, *Mariner 9,* was launched in 1971; its mission was to orbit Mars, photographing most of the planet's surface.

The previous U.S. Mars missions were relatively trouble-free, but not this 1971 mission. *Mariner 9's* sister craft was lost in the Atlantic Ocean on lift-off. During the months-long journey to the fourth planet, the planetary probe's thrusters began to leak, and its ability to change course and position was seriously reduced.

Despite these problems, the spacecraft arrived at Mars on November 18, 1971. The mechanical problems were at an end, but not the mission's troubles. *Mariner 9* turned its cameras Marsward, but those cameras showed nothing of the Martian surface, not even those features the previous Mariner probes had photographed. Filling the thin atmosphere of Mars was a planetwide dust storm through which nothing of the surface could be seen.

21

The storm continued to blow for several weeks, each day counting down to the end of *Mariner 9*'s electronic life. Finally, the storm ended, and as the dust settled, *Mariner 9* sent earthward its first surface pictures. They were pictures that once more transformed our ideas about the red planet, for out of the dust came not more craters but the summits of four giant volcanoes.

With the appearance of these peaks, present-day Mars study truly begins. It is a study based on the information sent back not only by *Mariner 9,* but also by NASA's 1976 Viking mission, as well as various Soviet craft. It is an ongoing study whose end is not even in sight.

2

THE GEOLOGY OF MARS

Mariner 4 sent back the first pictures of the Martian surface in 1965. In the quarter century since then, planetary scientists have learned a great deal about the fourth planet. Much of this information has come from spacecraft that actually visited Mars. *Mariner 9* photographed much of the Martian surface in 1971 and 1972. Even better photographs, as well as detailed information on atmosphere and soil, were sent back by NASA's *Vikings 1* and 2 in 1976. The Viking mission placed two craft in orbit around the planet and two landers on the surface. (The landing capsule of the Soviet Union's 1971 *Mars 3* probe was the first terrestrial craft to land on the fourth planet, but it ceased transmitting twenty seconds after touchdown.) The *Viking 1* lander continued collecting and sending information from the Martian surface for over six years.

Scientists have also learned about Mars through continuing telescopic examination. New devices such as the Charge-Coupled Device (CCD) improve the clarity of photos from telescopes. The CCD is a silicon chip that replaces the camera attached to the eyepiece of a telescope. It is more sensitive to light than film emulsion and records a more detailed image than any camera. The image is sent to a computer for storage and later recreation. During the close approach of Mars in 1989, CCD images gave astronomers some of the clearest views of the red planet ever recorded by Earth-based observatories.

Earth itself has given planetary scientists some of the best information about Mars. Many of the features seen on Mars have analogs on our planet. Look at Figure 4. First, one sees an orbital picture of the Martian surface, then an aerial view of desert terrain in the U.S. Southwest. They could well be the same region, but they are separated by millions of miles of space. By studying the processes that led to terrestrial formations, scientists have inferred much about Martian geology and climate.

ON THE SURFACE

Mars's southern hemisphere is a series of very old lava plains dotted with the remains of old meteorite craters. Although somewhat moonlike, it does not have mountain ranges like the Moon. A network of long, shallow channels cover this southern terrain. The southern polar cap is not, as *Mariners 6* and 7 reported, made up just of frozen carbon dioxide. Lying beneath its dry-ice surface is a deposit of frozen water. In the summer much of the frozen carbon dioxide, as well as some of the water, melts.

Mars's northern hemisphere is geologically younger than the southern. Portions of it are no more than a billion years old in contrast to the southern plains' 3 or 4 billion years. Unlike southern Mars, this hemisphere has fewer old meteorite craters and possesses immense canyon systems and a number of vol-

Figure 4. Do you think the Martian surface on the left resembles the desert terrain of the southwestern United States shown on the right?

canoes. Channels and valleys crisscross the northern surface. The northern polar cap, like the southern, is covered by frozen carbon dioxide, but its dry ice layer is thinner and in the summer melts completely. The northern cap has more water ice than the southern and is the largest known supply of water on the planet.

The northern and southern hemispheres almost seem like parts of two different planets, yet a quick glance at the Earth shows its northern and southern hemispheres to be just as different. Earth's northern hemisphere contains most of the landmass on the planet; the southern, most of the water. Such hemispherical diversity also exists on the Moon and Venus. No one knows why these differences exist.

One of the most extensively studied regions of Mars lies not far from the Martian equator, where large volcanoes preside at the head of a giant canyon. Four of these volcanoes, among the largest on Mars, sit on a plateau located just north of Mars's equator. Known as the Tharsis Bulge, this plateau is bordered on the northwest by the tallest known volcano in the solar system, Olympus Mons, meaning Mount Olympus. Olympus Mons dwarfs the largest volcanic mountain (and highest mountain) on Earth: Hawaii's Mauna Loa. The Martian volcano rears more than 15 miles (24 kilometers) above the surrounding plateau, while the Hawaiian peak rises only 5.6 miles (9.1 kilometers) from the sea floor. Olympus Mons's *caldera,* a bowl-shaped depression on its summit which could swallow all of Los Angeles, is a hundred times larger than that of Mauna Loa. A dozen Mauna Loas could fit within the bulk of Olympus Mons. (See Figure 5.)

Olympus Mons's true nature—its height, its breadth, its very character—was unknown until *Mariner 9*'s 1971 photographic survey of Mars. Was this massive mountain invisible to Earth-based telescopes? No, it wasn't—or at least, not quite. Olympus Mons was spotted as early as 1877 by the Italian astronomer Giovanni Schiaparelli. To him and to succeeding astronomers, however, the mountain appeared as nothing more than a very bright spot near the Martian equator. The Italian astronomer called this spot Nix Olympica (the Snows of Olympus). *Mariner 9* was not the first spacecraft to photograph Olympus Mons. In 1969 both *Mariners 6* and *7* photographed the Nix Olympica region as they flew by the planet. Their equipment was so crude that all they transmitted back

Figure 5. Olympus Mons, the largest known volcano in the solar system, showing its caldera at the top.

to earth was a photograph of a bright ring, which later turned out to be the rim of Olympus Mons's caldera.

Planetary geologists have learned much about the nature and history of Martian volcanoes by studying terrestrial examples. Olympus Mons, like the Hawaiian Mauna Loa, is a *shield volcano*. Such a volcano sends out slow flows of lava which creep out, covering previous lava beds. Over hundreds and thousands of years, this kind of volcano builds up a dome that from the air looks like a circular shield, giving this kind of volcano its name. Other than in height, Olympus Mons is quite similar in appearance to Mauna Loa.

27

Each volcano has a central caldera surrounded by a circular dome, its shield formed by lava from previous eruptions. Both have another characteristic of shield volcanoes, threads of lava radiating in all directions from the volcanic calderas. The Martian volcano, just like Mauna Loa, is a classic shield volcano.

Running southeast from the Tharsis Bulge is a canyon, Valles Marineris, the "Martian canyon." The orbital view in Figure 6 shows a portion of Valles Marineris, but this overhead view makes it look somewhat broad and flat. Stretching across a quarter of Mars's surface, this canyon is a gigantic fracture of it. Imagine a canyon 90 miles (150 kilometers) wide and 6 miles (10 kilometers) deep running from New York to Los Angeles. This would be Valles Marineris on Earth! This Martian canyon is the center of an extensive system of deep fractures in the Martian crust (the Grand Canyon would be nothing more than a side branch to this Martian rift). Earth has its equivalents to Valles Marineris. The remains of one such is the Great Rift Valley that stretches 4,000 miles (6,400 kilometers) from Jordan to Mozambique. Even larger rift valleys run from north to south along the length of both the Atlantic and Pacific seafloors.

THE SOIL OF MARS

Relatively little is actually known about the composition of Martian soil and rock. The soil, as analyzed by the Viking landers in 1976, is a hydrated (that is, water-containing) clay, while the rocks are volcanic in origin. The Vikings and the 1989 Soviet *Phobos 2* probe both demonstrated that Martian soil and rocks differ chemically from their counterparts on Earth. This difference is slight, but expected in light of the analysis of Moon rocks. Such rocks, returned to Earth by Apollo astronauts, also differ slightly from Earth

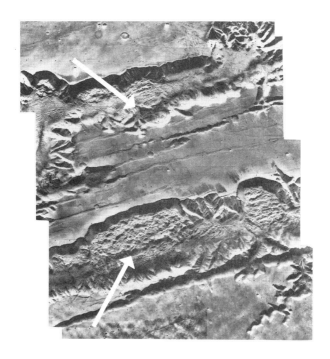

Figure 6. The arrows point to Valles Marineris, the Martian "Grand Canyon."

rocks. Mars's distinctive red color, however, comes from a compound common to both Earth and the fourth planet: iron oxide, the same thing as rust. On Earth, an iron-oxide-containing substance called hematite colors rocks red, but whether hematite exists on Mars is not known.

Both the United States and the Soviet Union have tentative plans to send automated probes to Mars to scoop up rock and soil samples for return to Earth, but planetary researchers may not have to wait for such missions. Scientists may already have found Martian rocks right here on Earth—in the Antarctic. Antarctica has revealed itself to be a treasure trove of meteorites. These meteorites, preserved in the ice for millions of years, are among the best such specimens ever collected.

Startling news came in 1984 when researchers announced that some of their samples were chemically identical to those Moon rocks collected by Apollo. Even more startling was the follow-up announcement that three of the rocks may have come from Mars. These three rocks held traces of gases such as nitrogen and neon. The ratio of the radioactive to nonradioactive forms of these gases was not that of Earth, but of Mars. Robert H. Carr of the Open University, Milton Keynes, England, discovered these ratios to be almost exactly the same as those found in the atmosphere of Mars by the Viking landers in 1976.

How did these rocks escape Mars and end up on Earth's southernmost continent? Smaller than Earth, Mars has a weaker gravitational field, only about 40 percent as strong as Earth's—a 150-pound (68-kilogram) human standing on Mars would weight only 57 pounds (26 kilograms). Debris thrown up by the powerful impact of a large asteroid would have enough velocity to escape the weak Martian gravity. Such an impact, however, would produce so much heat that this thrown material would partially melt. The Antarctic meteorites show no signs of such partial melting.

John D. O'Keefe and Thomas J. Ahrens of the California Institute of Technology, have determined by means of computer modeling, that an asteroid hitting Mars at an angle, rather than head on, could easily throw undamaged rocks out into space. Figure 7 shows the effect of such an impact. Friction from the atmosphere would heat the asteroid, and as this heat mounted, the asteroid would shoot out plumes of hot vapor. These vapor plumes would hit the Martian sur-

Figure 7. Plumes of superheated gas from an asteroid plowing through the Martian atmosphere at an angle may have hurled rocks into space. Three such rocks may have crossed the space between Mars and Earth and fallen in Antarctica.

face before the body of the asteroid and would dig up and hurl soil and rock off the planet, much as streams from high-pressure fire hoses send objects in their path flying down the street. Some of these scooped-up Martian rocks might well drift across space to fall through the Earth's atmosphere for a landing in Antarctica.

BENEATH THE SURFACE

In the last thirty years, geologists have come to recognize that the Earth's crust is made up of twelve large plates, as well as several smaller ones. These structures, called *tectonic plates*, float on hot, melted rock, known as *magma*. Currents in this supporting

31

magma carry each plate across the face of the planet. The hot rock beneath can sometimes escape to the surface at the edges of these plates. Such escaping magma forms volcanoes and becomes lava in the process. It eventually cools and hardens, adding to the rock on the surface.

Unlike Earth, Mars has a single, unbroken crust whose thickness of 125 miles (220 kilometers) is at least twice that of Earth's. No one can say for certain whether Mars has always had an unbroken crust or whether any tectonic plates it might have had fused as the planet cooled. The present-day planet, however, lacks any of the signs of tectonic-plate activity. On Earth, the most common mountains are those raised when two land masses on separate plates meet each other. As the plates collide, the land on them presses together and keeps pressing until soil and rock are forced up into a mountain range. The collision of the subcontinent India with Asia formed the Himalayas. Mars has not a single such mountain range, and it lacks any visible evidence that such mountains ever existed. Its only mountains are volcanic.

The very size of these Martian volcanoes may also be evidence that Mars's crust is not broken into tectonic plates. As Earth's tectonic plates drift, they carry continents, or parts of continents, toward or away from one another. No surface region on Earth will remain for more than a few million years over any one spot on the planet. Look at Figure 8. The drifting tectonic plate moves and carries its volcano away from the well of magma, the source of volcanic growth. As the plate drifts, wind and water erode away the bulk of the now-dead volcano. Many planetary scientists believe that a Martian volcano remains fixed over its magma source and continues growing, reaching dimensions impossible for earthly volcanoes. With a continuous supply of magma, it can easily replace material eroded by the

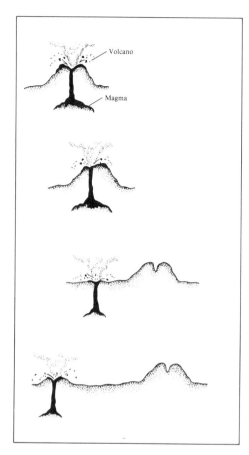

*Figure 8.
Tectonic plate
movement eventually
pulls terrestrial
volcanoes away
from the hot magma
that forms them.
Martian volcanoes
remain over the
source of their
magma and grow
much larger than
their counterparts
on Earth because
Mars has no
tectonic plate
movement.*

wind. Olympus Mons began forming some 1 billion years ago and had its most recent eruption about 100 million years ago. All the earthly mountain ranges and volcanoes formed during that period of Olympus Mons's growth are long gone, flattened by erosion or buried by newer mountains and volcanoes.

SHIFTING THE MARTIAN CRUST

For any one spot on Mars to drift away from escaping magma means that the whole crust, not just a portion of it as on Earth, has to move. Peter H. Schultz of Brown University believes that such movement has happened half a dozen times in the planet's 4.5 billion years' history. He thinks that some regions near the equator were once located at the Martian poles, but were moved to their present equatorial positions when the entire Martian crust shifted. The wandering of polar regions is common on Earth. Drifting tectonic plates have placed different sections of the surface beneath the Earth's North and South Poles. Antarctica now sits firmly on the South Pole, but at one time it was located to the north, where the temperatures were much warmer. Scientists have found fossils of everything from trees to dinosaurs as evidence of that more hospitable Antarctica. When Antarctica was basking in warmth, some other part of the Earth's surface was situated at the South Pole.

Schultz finds the evidence for his theory in Viking pictures of Mars's equator, which show some very unusual formations, unusual at least for the planet's equator. These formations are perfectly natural for the Martian poles. During the summer, melting polar ice reveals layered deposits lying beneath each ice cap. These layers are a mixture of ice and dust. In the Viking photos, Schultz has spotted similar layered deposits along Mars's equator. These equatorial deposits, although often badly eroded by wind, look very much like those under the present poles. Schultz is confident that such deposits can form only under polar conditions because new examples of this kind of layering appear nowhere else except at the poles.

Near these equatorial deposits are pedestal craters, meteorite craters sitting atop circular platforms. Such craters are unique to Mars and have posed a mystery for planetary scientists. Schultz believes that they are the product of polar migration. When an asteroid or meteorite strikes the ice cap, the object breaks through the icy surface. The force of the impact sends debris flying all around to form a layer over the surrounding ice. Much of this debris is dust from beneath the ice. Schultz points out that a warming—as would happen if the polar region drifted toward the equator—would melt all the ice surrounding the crater. Only ice lying under the impact debris would remain. This debris, being mostly dust, is unaffected by the rising temperatures and, acting as an insulating blanket, keeps the ice beneath it frozen. The result is a raised area or platform, the pedestal on which the crater sits.

What would cause the entire Martian crust to slip? Such slippage certainly must be difficult. Schultz says these infrequent crustal movements keep the planet balanced. At various times in the planet's history, it has had to move its crust to keep its rotation about its axis steady.

Take a ball and spin it. It spins smoothly and uniformly. Place a large wad of clay near its top and start the ball spinning again. The ball now wobbles because the clay makes the top slightly heavier than the bottom. Move the wad down toward the ball's equator, and the wobble decreases noticeably. A rotating planet is like that ball. It too is in danger of wobbling if part of its surface becomes heavier than another. To keep its balance, it shifts the troublesome section away from the pole and to the equator. Volcanic eruptions during Mars's history have spread lava unequally over various sections of the surface, and to keep the planetary rotation stable, the Martian crust has shifted, shoving the bulk of this material toward the equator.

Schultz claims that his theory of polar wandering also explains certain Martian features such as the steep slope or escarpment that circles the base of

Olympus Mons. Planetary geologists have advanced a number of ideas to explain the exisence of this escarpment (no such slope circles the base of Mauna Loa). Elliot Morris of the United States Geological Survey (USGS) thinks the escarpment formed because the Martian crust sagged under the weight of Olympus Mons. Others, such as Kenneth Tanaka of the USGS, think the formation is a large lava deposit that has been eroded by wind and water.

Peter Schultz, along with Carol Ann Hodges and Henry J. Moore, both of the USGS, points out that Olympus Mons's escarpment is easily explained if the mountain formed under the ice at Mars's north pole. For his evidence, he turns to Earth where such escarpments are found with shield volcanoes in Iceland. These Icelandic volcanoes initially erupted underneath an ice sheet and, after their hot lava burned through to the surface, continued erupting on the ice above. Schultz reasons that Olympus Mons's escarpment indicates the volcano formed at Mars's north pole. Schultz thinks that the mass of both Olympus Mons and the volcanoes of the Tharsis Bulge so disturbed the rotation of Mars that the entire crust shifted to move then closer to the equator.

Schultz also believes that the beginning of Valles Marineris came when the Martian crust shifted, stretching the surface to the breaking point. As with all planetary equators, that of Mars bulges because the planet's spin actually compresses the poles and expands the equatorial regions. Some 2 billion years ago Mars's crust made one of its infrequent shifts. The surface stretched and broke at one point as it moved across the equatorial bulge. Thus began Valles Marineris. The remainder of the canyon formed when the volcanoes of the Tharsis Bulge arose. Their eruptions fractured the surface in and around Valles Marineris until it achieved its full extent as seen today.

THE MARTIAN CORE

Planetary geologists suspect that the interior of Mars is colder than Earth's and that the Martian core is solid. They reason that Mars, being smaller than the Earth, would have lost internal heat more quickly and naturally cooled faster. Of even more importance is the absence of a strong Martian magnetic field. Earth, Jupiter, and Neptune all possess strong magnetic fields, and all have largely liquid interiors, while bodies such as Venus and the Moon have almost no magnetic field and have solid cores. The only information about Mars's magnetic field comes from the Soviets' *Mars 5* spacecraft. Before it died in orbit in 1973, this craft may have detected a weak magnetic field around the planet. *Phobos 2,* the only other probe designed to search for Martian magnetism, failed to find a magnetic field because its magnetometer proved inadequate for the task. Mars may or may not have a magnetic field, but if it does, it is a weak one. This lack of a strong field around the planet probably means that its center is cold and solid.

If the geologists' suspicions are correct, then Mars's active geologic life is largely behind it. Heat from the Earth's interior keeps our planet geologically active. A hot liquid mixture of nickel and iron at the Earth's core keeps the magma underlying the crust molten and is responsible for continuing volcanic activity such as that recently seen in Hawaii. Of equal importance is the heat produced by the decay of radioactive elements such as uranium and thorium.

No one, however, knows whether Mars still has significant heat in its interior and thus magma for more volcanoes. Both Viking landers were equipped with seismometers, instruments to detect quakes, volcanic eruptions, or other seismic activity. By comparing readings from both instruments, scientists hoped to discover whether the Martian core was still liquid. The experiment's success depended on both instruments' working, and unfortunately *Viking 1*'s failed. The search for radioactive elements was more successful. In 1971 the Soviet Union's *Mars 3* spacecraft detected the presence of uranium and thorium in the Martian soil in much the same concentrations as found on Earth.

Whether or not Mars is now a geologically dead world, scientists are still learning about the formation of the Mars we see. Many planetary geologists are convinced that water played a major role in sculpting the surface of Mars. The contemporary Mars may not have any free-flowing water, but in its past it may have been ravaged by the tearing torrents of giant floods.

3

THE WATERS OF MARS

The volcanoes rumble to the north of the underground cavern. Their almost constant lava flows are raising high domes. The magma shoots up the mountainous throats, and its heat seeps through the rocks to stir the already hot water in the underground reservoir. The water, partially frozen, churns and presses hard against the confining rock ceiling. The stressed rock groans and shudders under this liquid assault and suddenly breaks and collapses. Water roars out the opening. The torrent tears the exit wider, and pressed hard by the still-trapped water behind it, the wave front thunders across the surface, leaping high as it smashes and drowns rocks caught in its path. With ice chunks bobbing madly in its current, the flood's surface fizzes and hisses as it meets the cold, carbon dioxide–rich air. The released water rips and gouges deep, long channels in the surface rock within a few days, and far from its starting point, the flood spreads out into a shallow lake. The water begins to refreeze.

Some planetary geologists such as David Pieri of

the Jet Propulsion Laboratory (JPL) believe that such floods, erupting from underground reservoirs, crossed and recrossed the Martian surface thousands of times, perhaps as recently as 50,000 years ago. These raging waters left behind the deep, twisting channels and canyons of the northern hemisphere of Mars. Other evidence indicates that rain may have fallen on Mars 3 or 4 billion years ago. During that same period Mars may even have had a shallow sea.

A SCARCE COMMODITY

Michael H. Carr, a planetary geologist formerly with the Viking project and now with the USGS, believes that the young Mars had enough water to cover the entire planet to a depth of 1,500 feet (465 meters). Other estimates run as low as 3 feet (1 meter) and as high as 0.6 mile (1 kilometer). Even the lowest of these figures means a great deal of water, and Ronald Greeley of Arizona State University is confident that Mars once had all that water. He believes that repeated lava flows in Mars's past covered between 40 and 65 percent of the surface. So much volcanism would have been more than sufficient to produce the water necessary for the great Martian floods since water—whether on Earth or Mars—is a by-product of volcanic activity.

No water runs on Mars today, whatever may have been the case in the past. Liquid water can't exist on the Martian surface because the atmospheric pressure of Mars is so low that any exposed water would boil away immediately. The boiling point of water at sea level on Earth is 212 degrees Fahrenheit (100 degrees Celsius), but as altitude increases and atmospheric pressure decreases, this boiling point goes down. In Denver, 1 mile (1.6 kilometers) above sea level, water boils at 202 degrees Fahrenheit (95 degrees Celsius).

The atmospheric pressure on the surface of Mars is equivalent to a terrestrial altitude of 22 miles (35 kilometers) and is only 0.06 percent of the pressure at sea level on Earth. The boiling point of water at such a low atmospheric pressure is well below water's freezing point of 32 degrees Fahrenheit (0 degrees Celsius). When ice melts on Mars, it is already well above the boiling point of water. The northern ice cap doesn't melt in the summer: the water goes directly from ice on the ground to water vapor in the air.

Even ice is not found over the entire Martian surface. A belt that extends 30 degrees north and south of the equator is ice-free because temperatures are too high. The only form of water found in this equatorial region is water vapor. Solar radiation soon breaks down part of this vapor into oxygen and hydrogen, the latter of which rises to the top of the thin atmosphere, where it escapes into space. Some water is lost forever in this way from Mars. Wind carries the rest of the water vapor north or south, and as the temperatures drop, the water gas becomes ice.

Measurable quantities of water on present-day Mars, therefore, are small, even taking into account ice on the surface and water vapor in the atmosphere. Scientists have not discovered enough water on Mars for even a small flood, let alone thousands of immense torrents. Both poles have water ice, but neither one is very large, with much of the south polar cap being frozen carbon dioxide. Frost, as seen in photographs from the Viking landers, routinely covers parts of the Martian surface, but that icy layer is very thin. The air is dry, too, containing only 0.03 percent water vapor.

THE ARGUMENT FOR MARTIAN WATER

Present-day Mars may be a dry planet, but planetary geologists insist that the fourth planet must have had

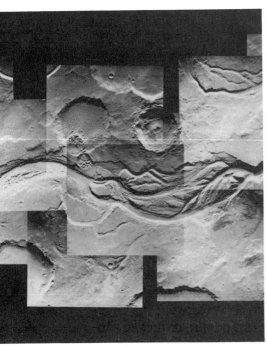

*Figure 9. Do you find any resemblance between
the branches of the Martian valley shown on the left
and the tributaries of the terrestrial
river shown on the right?*

a large volume of water sometime in its past. Michael
Carr points to pictures from the Viking orbiters. Figure 9 (left side) shows how many of the deep channels
in the northern hemisphere branch. To Carr, these
branches resemble the tributaries of terrestrial rivers
and streams (see right side of Figure 9).

Scientists see the evidence for Martian surface
water also in the southern hemisphere of Mars. Viking
photographs show shallow channels and gullies lacing
the southern surface, looking very similar to features
found in the desert of the U.S. Southwest. Those in

the terrestrial desert carry runoff from rain, and planetary geologists think the Martian channels may have once done the same on Mars. Could it actually have rained there once ? No one knows for certain, but the evidence seems to indicate that the fourth planet once saw rainstorms. Any rain on Mars was in the planet's distant past since these southern plains, the oldest sections of the planet, are 3 to 4 billion years old.

These channels and valleys, believed by the geologists to be ancient Martian watercourses, cross almost every part of the fourth planet's surface. The nineteenth-century Italian astronomer Giovanni Schiaparelli was convinced he had seen natural waterways crossing the Martian surface, which he called *canali,* the Italian word for "channels." The channels now known to exist on Mars may be *canali,* but they are not those of Schiaparelli. Even the largest is too small to be seen by telescope from Earth, and it took the powerful cameras of the *Viking 1* and *Viking 2* orbiters to discover those in the southern hemisphere.

MORE EVIDENCE

Planetary scientists have also found other formations resembling water-shaped features on Earth that indicate the role of water in Mars's past. Tear-shaped mounds rise out of the Martian plains and look very much like terrestrial islands whose sides were molded by flowing water. Carr and others also point to the evidence for *sapping* on Mars. On earth, groundwater (or ground ice) can undercut cliffs and bring them tumbling down: water seeps or bubbles up and carries away soil and rock. The process is slow, but eventually sapping pulls the very foundation out from beneath the cliff. The result is a landslide. Valles Marineris and other Martian canyons seem to be victims of sapping.

Whole sections of their walls are now slumping ramps of jumbled rocks leading down to valley floors.

The northern hemisphere also contains mysterious formations looking exactly like sandbars, the kind found off some ocean beaches on Earth (see Figure 10). Timothy Parker of JPL believes that these structures once rested in an ocean. Parker is convinced that at sometime in Mars's past—presumably when it was warmer, with a denser atmosphere—a shallow ocean covered 15 percent of the Martian surface. Parker points to those sandbars and then points to the prehistoric Lake Bonneville, which covered most of what is now Utah. This body of water, the size of Lake Michigan, was more inland sea than lake, and its waves rolled against its shores some 2 million years ago. Climatic changes eventually dried up most of Lake Bonneville and left the present Great Salt Lake and the Bonneville Salt Flats. More importantly, Bonneville's receding waters left wave-shaped sandbars that closely resemble those on Mars. These structures formed when flood waters washed debris into Lake Bonneville. Parker believes that floods swept soil and rock into that shallow Martian sea. When the sea dried up, it, like Lake Bonneville, left its own landlocked sandbars.

THE POWER OF WATER

Parker's sea was probably fed by rivers or streams, but no trace of them remains (if they ever existed). The visible Martian channels and valleys were not rivers or streambeds, and the slow, but relatively constant, flow of running water did not cut through the surface of Mars to form them. Instead massive floods, each flood slicing its way through the soil of Mars in a matter of days or weeks, were the creative agent. Would even the greatest flood tear out deep channels in hard rock

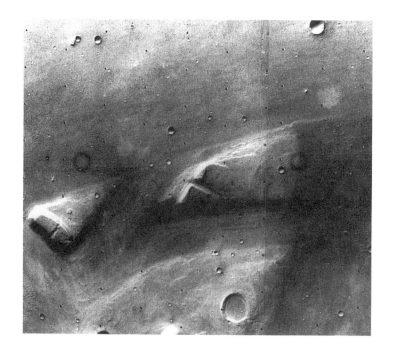

Figure 10. These sandbar-like formations may be evidence that Mars once had a shallow sea in its northern hemisphere.

so quickly? The planetary geologists say yes, explaining that water is a powerful force, whether in trickling streams or vast, roaring floods. A volume of water measured in cubic miles or kilometers is capable of causing such rapid erosion.

Geologists are not guessing about the effect of such floods. They have any number of examples right here on Earth. By studying these examples, they have come to understand—at least partially—the process of massive flooding on Mars. The channeled landscape of Mars and the channeled scablands of eastern Washington State look very similar. They look alike because, if planetary geologists are right, they were created by the same kinds of giant flooding.

Some 14,000 years ago, Lake Missoula, a huge lake, was fed by melting glaciers and covered much of what would become Montana and Idaho. The lake, penned at its western end by an ice dam, grew until the sheer weight of its water burst through the ice. A torrent of water exploded through the opening and swept in giant waves across the land. As it did so, it cut channels hundreds of feet or meters deep in a matter of days. The flood even changed the course of entire rivers. The lake level dropped rapidly and was soon below the broken ice dam, which then reformed. The whole cycle started over, and the Spokane floods continued until the glaciers retreated too far north for either lake or dam to survive.

Such catastrophic floods are rare on Earth, whereas on Mars they were once routine. The Martian floods were ten to a hundred times greater than any flood on Earth, and the source for their water was different from those that carved up eastern Washington. The water burst suddenly from underground caverns or rivers when the surface was broken by quakes or volcanic activity. For much of the planet's history, conditions on Mars prevented liquid water from running on the surface. The water of the torrential floods flowed for a short time because they were too deep and fast moving to freeze immediately. The flood waters did eventually freeze, as they spread and thinned out over the surface.

THE POWER OF ICE

Not all planetary geologists believe that liquid water eroded the surface of Mars. Some, such as Baerbel Lucchitta of the USGS, feel that ice, not running water, was responsible for surface erosion. Glaciers could have scooped out the deep valleys and canyons of Mars, just as, on Earth, ice-age glaciers scraped across large parts of the Northern and Southern hemispheres creating much of the rugged landscape of such places as New England and Scandinavia. A glacier, like a river, flows; it is a river of ice. Its movement is in feet or meters per year rather than feet or meters per minute as with a river, but its effect is the same: it moves soil and rock.

Lucchitta believes that glaciers might explain one of the peculiar features of some water-scarred areas on Mars. These odd regions are flat or else slope upward. Whatever flowed across them moved either on a flat surface or uphill. Water normally flows downhill, not up. Only water propelled by enough force—such as a Martian flood—flows uphill, but no matter what the driving force, this uphill movement is limited. Glaciers can move for long distances over flat or uphill terrain. The Wilkes subglacier in Antarctica, as Lucchitta points out, moved for 1,200 miles (2,000 kilometers) across a level plain.

Was Mars's surface carved by water or ice? Michael Malin of Arizona State University does not think a choice is necessary because he believes that both water and ice moved across the surface of Mars. During warmer periods in the planet's history, water may have caused such processes as sapping, but during colder times, ice would have been the eroding agent. A combination of water and ice may also have formed the channels and valleys of Mars since both forms could have been present in the same areas at the same time. Volcanic activity melting large underground deposits of ice could have produced some of the flooding.

Another possibility is that ice-covered streams might have flowed on Mars, particularly in the southern hemisphere. In some Antarctic valleys, lakes of water exist year-round—even through the coldest part of the winter. Layers of ice 15 feet (4.6 meters) thick cover each lake and keep the water from freezing. These ice lids remain even in the Antarctic summer. Streams flow into each lake during the summer, while during the winter, water evaporates from the icy surface and freezes to the icy bottom. Such freezing not only maintains the ice shield but also releases heat, keeping the lower water liquid. As long as summer streams replace that water lost to freezing and evaporation, the water beneath the ice remains fluid. The suspected runoff channels in Mars's southern hemisphere may have carried water protected by such icy lids. Such ice-capped channels may have emptied into craters, which, if also covered with thick ice, would have been just like the Antarctic lakes. These crater lakes could easily have kept a layer of water liquid even with surface temperatures far below freezing.

THE SEARCH FOR WATER ON MARS

Planetary geologists do not know where all the ancient Martian water has gone, but they suspect it is still on the planet. They admit that some water has been lost when its hydrogen, released by the action of solar radiation, escaped the planet, but they believe this loss to be small. Planetary scientist and consultant Bruce Cordell believes that Martian water exists in two places: first, as water in deep caverns 1 mile (1.6 kilometers) or more below the surface, and second, as ice just beneath the surface. Water on Mars would need to be far underground to remain liquid. In such deep reservoirs, it would be protected from freezing temperatures as well as being close to any possible internal heat.

Cordell believes that most of the water that did not go to fill his proposed reservoirs soaked into the surface to a depth of several hundred feet or meters and then froze. He thinks that this underground ice seldom exists as huge chunks but more often as small particles mixed in with the soil and rock of the planet's surface. Such a mixture of ice and soil is permafrost. Except for the polar caps, ice may not come any larger than a grain of sand on the fourth planet.

Stephen W. Squyres of Cornell University believes that permafrost is responsible for some odd meteorite craters on Mars. Martian impact craters are generally sharp-rimmed, angular-walled formations, just like those found on the Moon. Some craters on the fourth planet—those in the colder regions—have lost these edges so that they have broad rims and rounded walls. They look as though they have partially melted. Squyres believes that permafrost—ice mixed with crater rock—may be causing this distortion. The ice in permafrost, like the ice in glaciers, flows and, in flowing, carries along the particles of soil it surrounds. Ground on Earth with permafrost literally shifts (buildings are difficult to maintain on permafrost because this mobile substance pulls them down). If Squyres is correct, those odd-looking craters on Mars owe their appearance to the flow of permafrost.

Running water, seas, and lakes may have once existed on Mars, but none do now. The present Martian climate allows water to remain on or near the surface only as ice. Some planetary scientists argue that evidence for past surface water means that Mars once had a milder climate. Others believe that such surface water was a temporary phenomenon and that Mars's climate has remained virtually unchanged for billions of years. The climate of Mars today is harsher than any found on Earth, including that of Antarctica, which it most closely resembles. Its study, however, not only benefits from comparisons to Earth's climate, but also provides insights into terrestrial processes.

49

4

THE CLIMATE OF MARS

Much of what scientists know about the Martian climate comes from information sent back to Earth by spacecraft. The Viking landers alone transmitted three million weather reports between 1976 and 1980. Planetary researchers have used this data as well as a knowledge of terrestrial climate to build up a picture of the climate on Mars.

The Martian climate resembles that of Earth in certain basic ways. Mars's year has four seasons: spring, summer, fall, and winter. Surface temperatures are highest at the equator and lowest at the poles. Winds blow and storms move across the Martian surface. The fourth planet's sky has occasional white, wispy water clouds, and snow falls in the polar regions during the winter.

The Martian climate also differs from the climate of Earth. Each Martian season is longer than its terrestrial counterpart because Mars takes nearly twice as long to orbit the Sun as does the Earth. Mars also is colder than Earth because the red planet is about one and one-half times farther from the Sun and receives about half as much solar heat. Mars's average surface temperature is −9 degrees Fahrenheit (−23 degrees Celsius), while Earth's is +72 degrees Fahrenheit (22 degrees Celsius). The Martian winters are so cold that carbon dioxide freezes out of the air at the poles. No rain falls on the fourth planet, and the Martian sky is salmon-colored from suspended particles of dust. This airborne dust sometimes becomes a storm that blankets the entire sky, and as the scientists at JPL found out with *Mariner 9* in 1971, occasionally such a storm spreads until the surface of the whole planet is cut off from the sun.

THE SEASONS OF MARS

Mars has seasons for the same reason that Earth does. Its axis of rotation, the imaginary line that passes through the North and South poles and around which the planet rotates, is tilted from the vertical. The Martian axis of rotation tilts at an angle of 25 degrees, and as Mars orbits the Sun, first one hemisphere and then the other faces it more directly. The hemisphere pointing toward the Sun receives more solar heat than the one turned away. The northern hemisphere, therefore, experiences summer when it angles toward the Sun. The southern hemisphere, which points away from the Sun, undergoes winter. The reverse is true when the southern hemisphere angles toward the Sun and the northern away.

Mars's southern winter is much colder than its northern winter. The Martian South also has hotter summers than the North. Average winter temperatures in Earth's Northern and Southern hemispheres are very similar, as are their summer temperatures. Figure 11 shows the orbits of Mars and the Earth around the Sun. Mars can be as far as 155 million

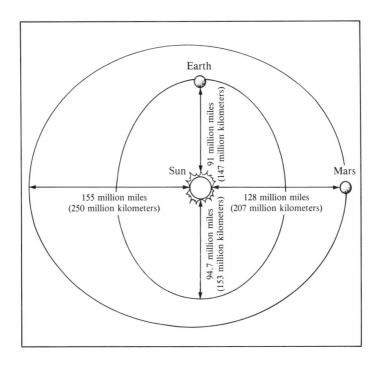

Earth

91 million miles
(147 million kilometers)

Sun

Mars

155 million miles
(250 million kilometers)

128 million miles
(207 million kilometers)

94.7 million miles
(153 million kilometers)

*Figure 11. Both Mars and Earth have a point in
their orbits where they are farthest from the Sun
and another where they are closest. The difference
between these two points is much greater
for Mars than for Earth.*

miles (250 million kilometers) from the Sun or as close
as 128 million miles (207 million kilometers). This is
a difference of 27 million miles (43 million kilometers). Earth's distance from the Sun varies by only 3.7
million miles (5.9 million kilometers). Mars's more ec-
centric orbit means that the Sun heats the two Martian hemispheres unevenly. Mars, when it is farthest
from the Sun, receives 40 percent less solar heat than
when it is making its closest approach. The far point of
Mars's orbit coincides with the southern winter and

the northern summer. The close approach comes during the northern winter and the southern summer. The southern hemisphere's winters are therefore both very cold and very long, while its summers are short and hot. The North experiences shorter and warmer winters and longer, cooler summers.

Mars is still a cold planet even during the southern summer. A particularly warm day can reach 80 degrees Fahrenheit (27 degrees Celsius), but summer daytime temperatures normally hover around the freezing point of water. Nighttime temperatures drop below zero degrees Fahrenheit or Celsius, and a difference of 180 degrees Fahrenheit (100 degrees Celsius) between day and night readings is not unusual in either hemisphere. Winter day and night temperatures in both hemispheres are always subzero. Mars's South Pole averages winter temperatures of -189 degrees Fahrenheit (-123 degrees Celsius), well below the freezing point of carbon dioxide, -109 degrees Fahrenheit (-78.5 degrees Celsius). Terrestrial temperatures, even in Antarctica, never approach these Martian South Polar lows. The coldest temperature, -128.6 Fahrenheit (-89 degrees Celsius), ever recorded on Earth was on July 22, 1983, at the Soviet Union's Antarctic research station Vostok.

THE GREENHOUSE EFFECT

Distance and orbit are not solely responsible for making Mars so cold. The planet's atmosphere is also a major factor because Mars has virtually no *greenhouse effect*. Heat from the Sun pours through Mars's atmosphere, as it does with Earth's, and hits the surface. The ground absorbs part of this heat, but the rest bounces back toward space. Mars's atmosphere allows practically all this spacebound heat to escape, while Earth's atmosphere permits only part to leave. Carbon dioxide and water vapor in Earth's atmosphere trap much of this surface-reflected heat and radiate it back toward the surface. The Earth's carbon dioxide and water vapor act just like a blanket or greenhouse that keeps plants warm in the winter. This insulating ability, called the greenhouse effect, was first proposed in 1973 by Carl Sagan and George H. Mullen of Cornell University.

Water vapor is present in the Martian atmosphere, but in amounts too small to establish any real greenhouse effect. Carbon dioxide makes up 96.5 percent of the Martian atmosphere, but the quantity is actually very small and is nowhere near enough for a greenhouse effect. Earth's atmosphere, which is only 0.03 percent carbon dioxide, has a far larger quantity of this gas than Mars.

THE WEATHER ON MARS

Mars's atmosphere is thin, only 0.6 percent as dense as the Earth's atmosphere. Atmospheric pressure at the surface averages 6.1 millibars of mercury, equal to the pressure found at 22 miles (35 kilometers) above the Earth. This pressure, as it does on Earth, drops with increasing altitude. The lowest point on Mars, the Hellas Basin, has a pressure of 8.4 millibars, while the highest, the summit of Olympus Mons, has a pressure of only 0.5 millibars. Atmospheric pressure on Mars varies considerably over the course of a year because the amount of carbon dioxide in the Martian atmosphere changes throughout the year. Winter temperatures, particularly in the southern hemisphere, drop so low that up to 30 percent of the gaseous carbon dioxide freezes out of the air. The surface pressure over the entire planet experiences a corresponding 30 percent drop. This frozen carbon dioxide

54

returns to the air when spring arrives and raises the planet's surface pressure.

The fourth planet's atmosphere is not so thin that winds do not exist on Mars. Martian winds are generally light breezes, moving at 2 feet per second (0.6 meter per second), but they can blow more strongly, sometimes reaching speeds greater than storm winds on Earth. They arise just as do winds on Earth. Warmer air rises and flows over adjacent colder, heavier air. The temperature of the air depends upon the temperature of the surface beneath it. The greater the difference in temperature between surface areas, the greater the wind speed.

These temperature differentials are greatest on Mars during spring at the edge of the southern ice cap. The intensely cold air above the ice cap and the much warmer air above the adjacent Sun-heated ground create fierce winds. Huge updrafts also occur as the Sun's heat turns the South Polar cap's frozen carbon dioxide back into a gas. The spring warming is particularly rapid in the South because Mars is making its closest approach to the Sun.

These conditions in the southern hemisphere lead to Martian dust storms. Such storms arise only during the southern spring, where the rapid heating of the ground and the pumping of large quantities of carbon dioxide into the air cause the strong winds and giant updrafts of air needed to carry dust high into the atmosphere. This dust often rises as high as 6 miles (10 kilometers). The plains of the southern hemisphere are also better suited for dust storms than the canyons and valleys of the northern hemisphere. (See Fig 12.)

Spring conditions in the South do not always produce dust storms. They sometimes generate dust devils, although dust devils that are miles high. Dust storms normally are confined to the southern hemi-

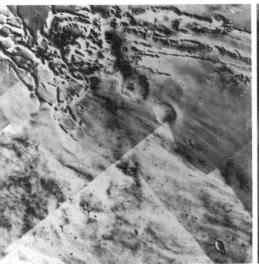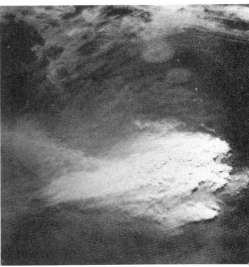

Figure 12. The photograph on the left clearly shows the Martian surface, which is hidden on the right by a dust storm. Such storms can spread until they blanket the entire planet.

sphere, but about every two years, high-altitude winds catch the rising grains of dust and carry them over the entire planet. Both localized and worldwide dust storms cut off much of the Sun's heat, and the surface beneath them cools rapidly. Such cooling eventually kills both winds and storms, but not before weeks or months have passed.

THE EVOLUTION OF MARTIAN CLIMATE

No one knows how long the present Martian climate has existed, but most planetary scientists agree it is at least 2 to 3 billion years old. The very early Mars, however, may have had a completely different climate. James F. Kasting of NASA's Ames Research Center has a computer model showing that Mars and Earth were very similar 4.5 billion years ago. Kasting believes that both planets were warm and had large quantities of gaseous carbon dioxide as well as liquid water. Mars had between 150 and 800 times as much carbon dioxide in its air as it does today. The two young planets then began a cycle that would produce much different results on Mars and Earth.

Water, released by volcanoes from each planet's interior, dissolved airborne carbon dioxide. Rain or snow carried the gas groundward, where it was bound into rocks. The process continued, and water washed most of the carbon dioxide out of the air of both planets. Continuing volcanism then melted some of the rocks containing the trapped carbon dioxide, releasing the gas back into the air for the whole cycle to begin again. This cycle kept a steady though small amount of the gas in the atmosphere of both planets. Enough carbon dioxide was present to produce the greenhouse effect, keeping average temperatures above the freezing point of water on both Earth and Mars.

This cycle of water, carbon dioxide, and rock still operates on Earth, but it stopped long ago on Mars. Mars's interior, according to Kasting's model, began cooling between 3.5 and 4 billion years ago. Volcanism decreased as the planet cooled, and the release of the trapped carbon dioxide dropped. Water still removed the gas from the Martian atmosphere, and as atmospheric levels of carbon dioxide decreased, Mars lost the protection of its greenhouse effect over the next 100 million years. Surface temperatures dropped until the fourth planet's liquid water froze, which finally ended the removal of carbon dioxide from the air. Most of Mars's trapped carbon dioxide remained trapped, and what little was released by the planet's remaining volcanoes was not enough to reestablish the greenhouse effect.

Kasting believes that the crucial difference between Earth and Mars was size. Mars, so much smaller than the Earth, lost its internal heat more quickly. Why is Mars smaller than the Earth? Peter Bodenheimer of the Lick Observatory of Santa Cruz, California, has used computer-generated models to study the way the solar system formed. These models show that Jupiter became so large that its immense gravitational pull yanked material out of the inner system. These stolen chunks robbed Mars of bulk, preventing it from becoming an Earth-sized planet. (Jupiter also pulled in so much material from the space between it and Mars that not enough matter remained to form a planet.)

What if Jupiter had been smaller, and Mars had grown to the size of Earth? James Kasting calculates that the fourth planet would have been earthlike, quite possibly habitable. Astronomers once thought the habitable zone, the region around a star where a planet like Earth could develop, was very small. An earthlike planet had to be within 93 million miles (150 million kilometers) plus or minus 5 million miles (8 million kilometers) of a star like our Sun to fall inside this zone. Kasting's work stretches this habitability zone to the orbit of Mars. Such a planet would be colder than Earth, but earthlike life could develop on it.

NUCLEAR WINTER

Mars may not be very earthlike today, but planetary scientists have learned much about Mars by studying Earth. They have also learned about processes on Earth from studying Mars. The Martian dust storms sparked one such investigation. These storms started scientists thinking about the way dust might spread and affect the Earth's climate. One source of such spreading dust is a nuclear explosion. Such explosions produce the familiar, ominous, mushroom-shaped cloud. The high-rising column is an immense updraft of air, carrying aloft not only radiation but also smoke and dust. The column rushes high into the air, where wind catches and stretches it out into the mushroom cap. As the smoke and dust spread farther, they become invisible to the human eye, but they are still there, circling high above the Earth's surface.

What, asked Carl Sagan and others, would happen if it were not just one blast over a relatively desolate test site? What would happen if nuclear war broke out? Sagan and his colleagues took the data on Martian dust storms and turned to their computers. The controversial answer was "nuclear winter." Computer models showed that, just like dust during a Martian storm, smoke, soot, and dust carried aloft by a large number of nuclear explosions would spread out, becoming a planetwide cloud. The Earth's surface, underneath this darkened sky, would be cut off from the Sun's heat and would quickly cool. How much the surface would cool is not clear, but it would be winter. This winter would cover the entire planet for weeks or months after an actual war.

Not only were the conclusions of Sagan and his group dramatic, but they quickly became the center of controversy. Other computer modeling produced different results, some even hinting at a "nuclear summer," and continuing study has led some scientists to challenge the concept of nuclear winter.

Other researchers, however, began thinking about ways, besides nuclear blasts, of generating updrafts to carry dust into the upper atmosphere. The late physicist Luis Alvarez and his son, geologist Walter Alvarez of the University of California at Berkeley, theorized that an asteroid hitting the Earth 65 million years ago threw millions of tons of water and dirt into the Earth's upper atmosphere. Winds spread the water and dirt into a planet-shrouding cloud that triggered a worldwide winter, which then killed off the dinosaurs. Other sources for a worldwide dust storm are violent volcanic eruptions. The August 27, 1883, eruption of the Indonesian volcano Krakatoa threw 5 cubic miles (21 cubic kilometers) of matter 50 miles (80 kilometers) into the air. Ash from Krakatoa blotted out the Sun for two and one-half days in the nearby region, and fine dust from the eruption circulated in the upper atmosphere for three years.

LOCATING THE ANCIENT MARTIAN ATMOSPHERE

James Kasting's model of Mars depends upon the planet's having had more water and carbon dioxide than is presently detectable. Planetary scientists are, of course, searching for that suspected water. They are also looking for the missing carbon dioxide. They have searched the Viking photographs of the planet's surface for signs of rocks that might hold the carbon dioxide of Mars's past. They have not seen any such rocks, but since most carbon-containing rocks on Earth are buried under the surface, many planetary geologists expect that Mars's supply will also be found underground.

Ted L. Rousch of Ames believes differently after examining Mars with an infrared telescope. Infrared radiation is invisible, lying just beyond the red part of the visible spectrum. We feel it as heat. All matter gives off infrared radiation, and objects and material that are invisible to a standard telescope can often be spotted using an infrared telescope. Rousch's infrared observations of Mars found traces of carbon dioxide in the dust floating in the fourth planet's air. Rousch believes that most of the ancient Martian atmosphere is literally lying on the planet's surface trapped in dust particles, which are quite porous and absorbent.

The search for the missing carbon dioxide will continue along with the search for Mars's water. Finding both is crucial to knowing whether Mars ever was the dynamic young planet James Kasting pictures. Kasting's young Mars would have had running water, rainfall, and lakes, perhaps even a shallow sea. The young Earth possessed all these elements, and the result was life. The young Mars may also have produced life.

5

LIFE ON MARS

One of the major purposes of the 1976 U.S. Viking mission was to search for life on Mars. Both of the landers were equipped with small automated biological laboratories designed to run Martian soil through several tests. Biologists hoped that these tests would reveal whether or not Mars had microorganisms—small animals, plants, fungi, or bacteria visible only with a microscope. NASA thoroughly sterilized the Viking spacecraft prior to launch from Earth to ensure that they would not bring terrestrial life to the fourth planet.

THE VIKING TESTS

The two landers set down on the surface of Mars six weeks and 3,100 miles (5,000 kilometers) apart in the summer of 1976. Each lander's cameras were immediately turned on to see if anything was actually crawling around near it (this was a serious test). The landers then scooped up Martian soil for processing by their biological labs (Figure 13). One of the tests called

Figure 13. The Viking 1 *lander used a mobile arm to collect soil samples for biological experiments.*

for a sample of soil to be placed in a nutrient solution. Any microscopic plants present would use this solution in photosynthesis, a process that would produce food for the plant and oxygen as a by-product. The test looked like a success when oxygen did eventually bubble out of the soil sample. Another test also gave promising evidence of Martian life. One of the soil samples was exposed to radioactive carbon dioxide in the hopes that any microorganisms in the soil would absorb some of the gas. Radioactive carbon dioxide was indeed found in the soil sample after several days. A third soil sample was heated to kill any possible life and then also exposed to radioactive carbon dioxide. The amount of the radioactive gas taken up by the soil was considerably less than with the unheated sample, as was to be expected if the carbon dioxide absorption was mostly a biological effect.

The Viking landers, despite these seemingly positive results, had not found Martian life. The landers followed up their biological testing with a search of the Martian soil for the actual carbon-containing chemicals of life such as proteins (complex carbon chains that are the building blocks of living things) and DNA (the material that makes up genes). They found nothing. They even failed to find simpler but essential chemicals such as amino acids, the separate units composing proteins. More tests followed, and the scientists concluded that the results of the three tests were not evidence for Martian life. Nonliving processes were responsible for the oxygen production and the carbon dioxide absorption. Mars was a dead world for Viking.

THE DEADLY SURFACE OF MARS

The failure of the Viking tests does not eliminate the possibility of life on Mars. Martian life may be in a form not found on Earth, or it may simply be at some other location than that examined by the landers. Life, as we know it on Earth, exists in the harshest of terrestrial environments such as Antarctica. The Martian environment, however, is much more hostile than the terrestrial environment and provides fewer places where life could survive. Most biologists do not consider the Martian surface to be one of those places, and they believe that any possible life on Mars lives underground.

The Martian surface is cold and dry and bombarded daily with massive amounts of ultraviolet radiation (UV) from the Sun. UV is the same radiation that tans human skin. It can cause skin cancer. Mars has no barrier to the Sun's UV such as Earth has, with its high-altitude concentration of ozone, known as the ozone layer. Ozone is related to oxygen, but where the latter has two oxygen atoms, the former has three. Mars, with almost no oxygen in its air, has no ozone and no ozone layer to act as a UV filter. This unblocked UV creates peroxides from the oxygen found in the iron oxide of the Martian surface. Hydrogen peroxide is a common disinfectant used here on Earth, and these UV-created peroxides in the Martian soil act just like a superdisinfectant poured over the entire outside of the planet. Any possible Martian life, if it is similar to terrestrial life, could not survive.

Mars's lack of an ozone layer emphasizes the importance of such a shield for living things on Earth. Scientists have detected a measurable drop in the density of the Earth's ozone layer due, they believe, to chlorofluorocarbons. These chlorofluorocarbons, used in aerosol sprays, air conditioners, and refrigerators, chemically attack and destroy ozone in the Earth's upper atmosphere. Researchers have recently discovered large holes in the ozone layer that have formed over both the North and South poles. If the ozone layer should continue disappearing, humans as well as every other living thing on Earth will be exposed to higher and higher levels of ultraviolet radiation.

UNDERGROUND LIFE

Microorganisms living a few feet or meters beneath the Martian surface would probably be safe from the effects of UV-created peroxides. They, or larger life forms, might also find protection in caves, but any underground Martian life would be cut off from the Sun. Biologists once thought that all life derived its energy from sunlight. Green plants on Earth turn sunlight into food for themselves. Then animals eat the plants, feeding on recycled solar energy, and finally, other animals eat these plant eaters. The energy that carnivores derive from eating other animals is still from the Sun, even if thirdhand. In 1979 John Baross, an oceanographer at Oregon State University, found life living 1.5 miles (2.5 kilometers) beneath the Pacific Ocean on the Central Pacific Ridge. The ridge is in perpetual darkness since sunlight penetrates ocean water to only 600 feet (185 meters).

The life Baross discovered was a whole population of organisms clustered around hot-water vents (Figure 14). The area was covered with clamlike animals and worms 5 feet (1.5 meters) long. In the hot water surrounding the vents were bacteria. How do these creatures survive without the Sun to provide them energy? They have another source of energy, geothermal energy, which is heat generated by volcanoes or hot springs. This deep-sea colony—and others that have been found in the Atlantic—replaces the Sun with a hot-water vent. Such vents are similar to the geysers of Yellowstone National Park. Biologists are still learning how these creatures use geothermal energy, but they know that the bacteria convert sulfur from the hot water into food and then become food for the larger animals.

Figure 14. Strange creatures live around hot-water vents deep in the oceans on Earth. Perhaps similar formations and creatures exist in underground reservoirs on Mars.

Creatures similar to these Pacific ridge organisms might live deep within Mars. Planetary scientist and consultant Bruce Cordell believes that much of Mars's missing water is located in caverns far beneath the surface and that the planet's remaining internal heat keeps this water from freezing. Such natural reservoirs might well have hot-water vents, and living around those vents might be Martian organisms that survive on geothermal energy.

EARLY LIFE ON MARS

Many biologists, even those who believe that the conditions on Mars and the Viking's findings mean that nothing is alive on the fourth planet today, do not rule out the possibility that the red planet may harbor the remains of life that arose and flourished on Mars several billion years ago. Surface temperatures during Mars's first half billion years (between 4 and 4.5 billion years ago), though low, may have been higher than those that came later. Michael H. Carr of the USGS believes that the climate of the early Mars was similar to that now found along the North Slope of Alaska in winter. Some terrestrial organisms live quite comfortably in this region (Figure 15). Robert Wharton of the Desert Research Institute in Reno thinks that even colder Mars might have supported life. This life might have evolved and lived in ice-covered lakes, just like the algaelike creatures that swarm in the protected waters of the ice-capped lakes in Antarctica. The pigments that give these Antarctic organisms their red, green, and purple colors also take sunlight that filters through the thick ice shield and make food out of it. Similar creatures could well have lived in ice-covered craters in the southern hemisphere of Mars. These crater lakes would have provided the liquid water and the sunlight needed for life.

The cool temperatures of the early Mars would have given way to periods of intense heat. The fourth planet, like the young Earth, was bombarded by debris, including large asteroids, left over from planetary formation. The impacts produced great quantities of heat, and asteroids that bored deeply enough released hot magma from underground. The young Mars would have alternated between hot and cold, giving rise to conditions that might have been suitable for the formation of life. David Deamer of the University of Cal-

Figure 15. Life might have evolved and lived in ice-covered Martian lakes, just as algae seems to flourish in some of the icy waters in Antarctica.

ifornia at Davis believes that such alternating hot and cold periods brought forth life on Earth.

Deamer says that rapid cycles of hot and cold, wet and dry, provided the necessary motive power to change nonliving chemicals into living things. Deamer believes that life arose many times in the first billion years of Earth's history and that life first appeared in isolated tidal pools. Each pool contained all the ingredients of life such as DNA and proteins, but when the pool dried, the creature died. These early organisms eventually developed ways to enclose themselves. Thus, they survived the disappearance of their pools and became the ancestors of all present life on Earth.

The young Mars might have seen much the same evolutionary process. Martian DNA may have formed and pulled together amino acids to make proteins in small pools along the shore of a shallow sea in Mars's northern hemisphere. Martian life-forms may have migrated from these tidal pools to the nearby sea. Then, when Mars began to cool and the sea began to evaporate and freeze, they may have found shelter in ice-covered craters. Such life eventually would have died when liquid water disappeared forever from the Martian surface. Its fossilized remains may be awaiting human explorers or their machines in the bottoms of those old craters.

MARTIAN FOSSILS

What will these fossils consist of? They probably will not be preserved footprints or frozen bodies. They probably won't even be animal bones or plant bodies that have turned to stone. Most likely these remains will be a buried layer of organic matter. This organic material will probably reveal its nature in the ratio of nonradioactive carbon (carbon 12) to radioactive carbon (carbon 13). On Earth, this carbon 12/carbon 13 ratio is higher for living things than for nonliving carbon-containing material such as rocks. Biologists expect that these ratios will probably be the same on Mars.

Scientists may not have to wait for another landing on Mars to find Martian fossils. They may already be on Earth, held within one of those three meteorites found in Antarctica and thought to have originally formed as rocks on Mars. In 1989, Ian P. Wright of the Open University in Milton Keynes, England, discovered two types of carbon-containing chemicals in one of these Mars rocks. One type proved to be nonliving material, while the other showed the carbon 12/carbon

13 ratio expected of life-forms. Has Wright found the fossilized remains of Martian life? He hopes so. However, John F. Kerridge, a chemist at the University of California at Los Angeles, warns that the meteorite may have been contaminated by material from Earth. Further tests may yet tell reseachers whether Martian life has been discovered.

NASA sterilized the Viking landers to prevent contamination of Mars with terrestrial life, but life-forms from Earth may already have made the trip to Mars. These terrestrial organisms may have made the trip on terrestrial rocks that, like those suspected Martian rocks, found their way across millions of miles of space. S. A. Phinney of the University of Arizona has created a computer model that shows the course of a thousand rocks tossed off the Earth's surface by an asteroid hit. Almost half these rocks were lost in space, and a third ended up on Venus, but seventeen of them made it to Mars. Such rocks in reality might well have carried bacteria to Mars and might have arrived before Martian surface water disappeared. The bacteria, with water available, might have adapted even to the arctic conditions of a dying Mars, and fossils on Mars may be of these terrestrial life forms and their descendants.

THE MOONS OF MARS

The first humans on Mars may find the night sky a strange sight with its two tiny moon disks. Phobos, the larger inner moon, would appear from the surface to be less than half the size of the full Moon, while Deimos, the smaller outer satellite, would be seven times smaller. These space travelers might not be able to see Deimos without a telescope, and they would find that neither moon is visible at either Martian pole. The strangest sight of all might be Phobos's crossing of the night sky. This moon would not only shoot across the night sky in five and a half hours, but it would rise in the west rather than the east.

Phobos and Deimos, the two moons of Mars, are small, irregular-shaped objects difficult to study from Earth because they are so tiny. Relatively little is known about these moons even more than a century after their discovery, and astronomers did not even know what they looked like until spacecraft photographed them in the 1970s. Their very size made them difficult to discover in the first place.

DISCOVERING THE MOONS OF MARS

Astronomers began using telescopes just after 1600, but for two and three-quarters centuries these instruments were not powerful enough to spot Phobos and Deimos. Several people claimed, however, to have discovered the moons of Mars during this period. The first such claim was actually due to a misunderstanding. The German astronomical pioneer Johannes Kepler received a letter in 1610 from his contemporary Galileo, who had recently discovered the four largest moons of Jupiter. The letter contained an anagram, and in the transposed letters and words of the puzzle was information on another astronomical discovery that Kepler thought referred to Mars. Kepler's interest in Mars had already led him to formulate the first of his three famous laws of planetary motion: that planets travel in elliptical orbits with the Sun at one focus of that ellipse. However, he mistakenly thought Galileo's anagram meant that the Italian scientist had seen two moons orbiting Mars, and he mentions this discovery in his 1610 book *Narratio de Jovis Satellitibus* ("Narrative of the Jovian Satellites"). Galileo's message actually referred to the rings of Saturn, which his primitive telescope had shown as two bright spots to either side of Saturn. Galileo thought these bright spots were two of Saturn's moons. Mars's actually having two moons was coincidence.

Many astronomers of the period were aware of Kepler's error, but not all. A Capuchin monk Anton Maria Schyrl said that in 1643 he had seen the two moons of Mars. Schyrl's telescope was no better than any other of the time, and he probably mistook two stars for Martian moons. The two objects he saw were not Phobos and Deimos, which would have been totally invisible to the telescopes of both Galileo and Schyrl.

Jonathan Swift, having read Kepler's *Narratio de Jovis Satellitibus*, has a character in *Gulliver's Travels*, published in 1727, who describes the discovery of two Martian moons. Swift may or may not have been aware of Kepler's mistake, but many readers, unaware of the Kepler book, have made much of Swift's description. They have assumed that he knew about Phobos and Deimos before their actual discovery, and they have labeled him as everything from a Martian to a psychic for his "predicting" that Mars had two moons.

Astronomers for the next 150 years actively searched for the moons of Mars. A half dozen people said they had seen one or more moons circling Mars, but all of these sightings proved to be either fakes or mistakes. No one succeeded in finding Phobos and Deimos until the American astronomer Asaph Hall spotted them in 1877.

OBSERVING THE MOONS OF MARS

Astronomers had difficulty in observing Mars from Earth, and they found it even more difficult to study the Martian moons. They learned little more than each moon's orbit and rotation. Phobos, the inner moon of Mars, orbits 5,830 miles (9,380 kilometers) above the planetary surface. It takes seven and one-half hours to make one complete revolution of Mars and makes three revolutions of the planet each Martian day. Deimos orbits Mars in thirty hours at an altitude of 14,600 miles (23,500 kilometers).

Phobos travels much faster than Mars rotates because the moon is so close to the planet's surface. The closer an object is to a planet, the faster it moves around that planet. The space shuttle, which normally orbits the Earth at an altitude of a little over 100 miles (160 kilometers) makes one orbit every ninety minutes, while the Moon, which is 238,000 miles (384,000 kilometers) away, takes a month. Most satellites of rotating planets are far enough out so that they travel more slowly than the planet rotates. They are overtaken by the sunrise line on the planet and appear on the planet's surface to rise in the east and set in the west. This is the case with the Earth's moon and Mars's Deimos. Phobos moves faster than the planet's spin and consequently overtakes the sunset line. To an observer on the planet, it appears to be rising in the west and setting in the east. The space shuttle, as well as artificial satellites orbiting at altitudes of a few hundred miles or kilometers, rise in the west in Earth's sky. On Mars, Phobos would appear first in the western sky.

The two moons spin on their axes. The rotational period for each moon is exactly the same as its orbital period, seven and one-half hours for Phobos and thirty hours for Deimos. Both satellites keep one face toward Mars at all times, just as the Moon does with Earth.

Future space travelers would have a poor view of Deimos from Mars because it is small and far away, but on Deimos they would have a spectacular view of the fourth planet. Mars, twenty times the size of the full Moon, would hang like a giant relief globe. The astronauts would be able to see all the major features such as Olympus Mons and the Hellas Basin.

These future Mars visitors may find the view of Mars from Phobos even more impressive, perhaps even frightening. The fourth planet would spread like a vast platter across the sky. The astronauts might even have the impression that Phobos is falling toward Mars, and they would be right. Phobos is in fact dropping toward Mars, although that drop is so slow that no human eye can detect it. British astronomer Anthony Sinclair of LaPalma Observatory in the Canary Islands has confirmed Phobos's fall. Sinclair's measurements show that over the past ten years Phobos has drawn 14 inches (36 centimeters) closer to Mars.

The scientist calculates that the inner moon of Mars will break up in the Martian atmosphere within the next 100 million years. Phobos's fragments will then plunge to the surface, adding a few new craters to the Martian terrain.

Phobos's impact may not be the first time a fragmenting moon has hit Mars. Mars has a type of impact crater found only at its equator. Such craters have a distinctive debris layer surrounding them. This layer, thrown out upon impact, looks like the wings of a butterfly. Donald E. Gault and John A. Wedekind of NASA's Ames Research Center believe that only an object in a close equatorial orbit—a moon or its fragments—could make such craters. If Gault and Wedekind are correct, Phobos will make more such butterfly craters when it hits the Martian surface.

Deimos will not share Phobos's fate. Mars's gravity, instead of dragging the outer moon down, is pushing the smaller satellite away. Deimos will eventually be free of Mars if this outward movement continues.

CLOSE-UPS OF PHOBOS AND DEIMOS

Astronomers have learned most of what they know about Phobos and Deimos from the various space probes that have visited Mars in the last twenty-five years. In 1969 *Mariner 7* photographed the shadow of Phobos on the surface of Mars, and in 1972 *Mariner 9* sent back the first picture of this Martian moon. The Viking orbiters photographed both Phobos and Deimos. The pictures show that Phobos and Deimos are potato-shaped. Phobos, measuring 17 miles (25 kilometers) along its longest axis, is almost twice the size of Deimos, whose maximum length is 8 miles (13 kilometers). The surface of Phobos is covered with craters and long, low-lying ridges. Long grooves that may be fracture lines from asteroid impacts cut across the moon's surface. Astronomers once thought Phobos's surface to be a uniform gray, but photographs made in 1989 by the *Phobos 2* spacecraft reveal red and blue patches. *Phobos 2* stopped operating before it could discover what these colored patches are. Phobos's surface is relatively free of debris because it is so close to Mars. Material thrown up by asteroid impacts has enough velocity to escape the weak gravity of Phobos, but not Mars's gravitational field. The planet, acting like a planetary vacuum cleaner, catches and sucks all this debris down to its surface.

A large crater named Hall, after the moon's discoverer, sits directly at the South Pole of Phobos. Stickney, an even larger crater that is 6 miles (10 kilometers) across, is located on the side of Phobos that always faces Mars (Figure 16). Planetary geologists think it likely the force of the collision that formed Stickney was so great that even the interior of Phobos is cracked. Phobos could well shatter if another major asteroid hit it. The fragments from such a breakup would form a short-lived ring around Mars.

Deimos is just as crater-pocked as Phobos, but a layer of dust covers and partially hides most of these depressions (Figure 17). House-sized boulders, casting long shadows, project above Deimos's dusty surface. The dust comes from material thrown up by asteroid impacts. Such impact debris initially escapes Deimos's weak gravity, but it is not pulled down to the Martian surface because Deimos is too far from Mars. The debris instead expands into a cloud that floats in Deimos's orbit. Deimos passes through this cloud of fragments on each of its revolutions around the planet, and with each orbital passage, part of this cloud settles to the moon's surface, coating the entire moon in dust.

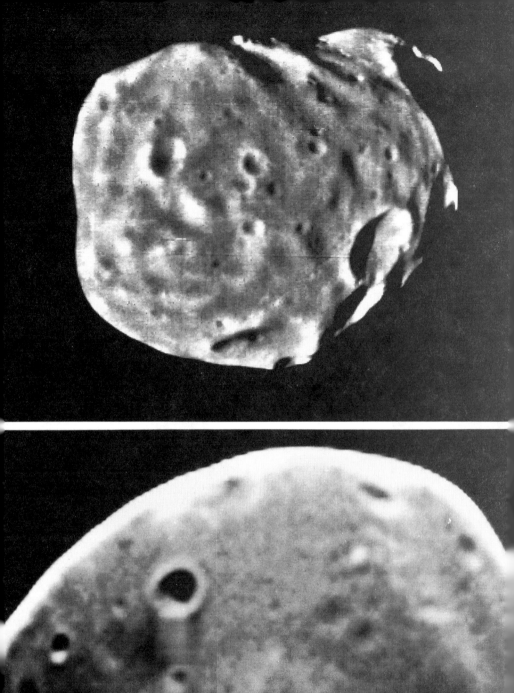

CAPTURED ASTEROIDS?

Little is known about the composition of the two Martian moons, but astronomers believe that both Phobos and Deimos may contain water and organic (carbon-containing) compounds such as methane. The two moons are similar in appearance to certain asteroids, called carbonaceous chondrites, that are known to have water and organics.

Some astronomers believe that Phobos and Deimos bear more than a close resemblance to asteroids. They suggest the two Martian moons are captured asteroids and not true moons at all. These scientists point to the smallness of the two satellites, particularly when compared with the size of the Earth's moon, and to the potato shape that is a common feature among asteroids (some asteroids such as Ceres are actually larger than either Phobos or Deimos).

Most astronomers believe it unlikely that Phobos and Deimos are captured asteroids because such captures are not easy, even for a giant such as Jupiter. A small planet like Mars probably could not capture one asteroid, let alone two. Neither Venus nor Earth, despite each planet's being almost twice the size of Mars, has even one such captive.

Why are Phobos and Deimos so small? Ganymede, a moon of Jupiter, is larger than the planet Mer-

Figure 16. Top: Phobos, the larger of Mars's moons, has numerous impact craters, of which Stickney (lower right) is the largest.
Figure 17. Bottom: dust covers the surface of Deimos, the smaller of Mars's moons.

cury, and Saturn's moon Titan and Neptune's Triton are almost as large. Such comparisons are deceptive. A more revealing comparison is that between these moons and the planets they orbit. Ganymede next to Jupiter does not appear much larger than Phobos next to Mars, and neither do Titan and Triton when compared to Saturn and Neptune. Mars, like most other planets in the solar system, has moons much smaller than itself. Only the Earth and Pluto, among the nine known planets, have satellites that are more than one-fourth the size of the planet they orbit. The origin of the Moon still baffles astronomers, but the Moon is large enough that some astronomers consider it to be a planet and the Earth-Moon duo to be a double planet system. Pluto and its moon Charon are even more of a mystery. They may be two parts of a once larger planet, or they may be two escaped moons of Neptune. Both the Earth-Moon and Pluto-Charon pairs are unusual in the solar system.

RENDEZVOUS WITH PHOBOS

The Soviet Union launched its two Phobos spacecraft in 1988 to try and learn more about Phobos, particularly its composition. The mission called for one craft to photograph Phobos's surface from a height of 100 feet (30 meters), and the other was to vaporize a section of that surface with a laser and analyze the result. A small lander was to set down on Phobos as a final step. This landing would be a delicate maneuver since Phobos's surface gravity is so small (anyone who can jump 3 feet (1 meter)—straight up—could break free of Phobos's gravity). The lander, after touchdown, was to anchor itself by shooting a harpoon into the ground to keep it from floating back into space.

The mission was only a partial success. *Phobos 1* never made it to Mars. A ground controller's error turned its solar energy collectors away from the Sun, and after its batteries were drained, it died. *Phobos 2* did reach Mars on February 5, 1989, but stopped sending signals after only two months. It did transmit a great many orbital pictures of Phobos, as well as doing several photographic surveys of the Martian surface. It did not last long enough to conduct the surface survey or the laser test, nor was it able to put its lander on the surface of Phobos.

The possible existence of water on Phobos was one of the major reasons for the Soviet's Phobos mission. If the moon does have water, as suspected, it may have a crucial role to play in any future human exploration of Mars. The crew of a Mars ship could manufacture liquid oxygen and liquid hydrogen, rocket fuel, from such water. The crew's ability to make this fuel in orbit around Mars would mean their ship would not have to carry fuel, a bulky item, for the return trip. Other supplies such as food, medicine, scientific instruments could replace that return-trip fuel. Mars itself might have the necessary water for such fuel, but that water—or the fuel made from it—would have to be lifted into orbit for use. Water on Phobos would be right where the spaceship is.

Phobos 2 found only a trace of water on Phobos's surface. The probe's search for water, however, was both incomplete and confined to the moon's surface, and U.S. scientists Fraser P. Fanale and James R. Salvail of the University of Hawaii still believe Phobos has water. The two planetary scientists theorize that the water lies beneath the moon's surface. They have created a mathematical model of the evolution of Phobos, and their calculations indicate that water should lie just below the surface at the moon's poles, although it may be as much as 0.6 mile (1 kilometer) deep in Phobos's equatorial region. *Phobos 2* did discover that the density of Phobos was much less than previously thought. This finding fits with Fanale and Salvail's theory since interior ice could account for Phobos's lower density.

Much still remains to be learned not only about Phobos and Deimos but also about Mars, and whether or not Phobos proves to be a source of rocket fuel, *Phobos 1* and 2 will probably not be the last visitors to the fourth planet. Both the United States and the Soviet Union are planning and preparing a number of future missions, and not all of these projects depend upon automated spacecraft.

7

THE BECKONING LURE OF MARS

Planetary scientists have learned a great deal about Mars in the last twenty-five years, but they also know better than anyone else just how much still remains to be learned about the fourth planet. Mars is a world whose surface area is larger than the entire exposed land of the Earth, and scientists have literally only scratched the surface of the red planet. Both the United States and the Soviet Union have missions planned for the further exploration of Mars. The first of these missions is the U.S. *Mars Observer*.

THE MARS OBSERVER
AND VESTA

The *Mars Observer*, unlike Viking with its two landers and two orbiters, will be a modest mission. It will be a single orbiter, whose cost is low because NASA will construct it out of preexisting parts. The probe's body will be a modified communication satellite shell, and its electronics will be the same as the units used in weather satellites. (See Figure 18.)

*Figure 18. The U.S. Mars Observer
is scheduled for launch in 1992.*

The *Observer* was originally scheduled for launch from the space shuttle in 1990, but the explosion of the *Challenger* delayed the mission. NASA hopes that it can begin its journey to Mars in 1992 atop a *Titan 3* rocket. The *Observer* will take up a polar orbit upon arrival at the fourth planet and will spend two years mapping every section of the planet. It will carry seventeen different instruments, some of which will search for a Martian magnetic field and probe for subsurface ice and water. One of these instruments will be a camera capable of making the most detailed and sharpest pictures of Mars yet. This camera will be twenty times as powerful as those mounted on the Viking orbiters. Another of the *Observer*'s instruments will be an altimeter with which to determine the exact heights and depths of surface features on Mars. The Viking orbiters lacked such altimeters, and planetary geologists have had to estimate Martian elevation by using overlapping photographs of the various formations. The data from the *Observer* will end the need for this practice.

The *Mars Observer* will complete its planetary work in late 1995, and as it does, another robot probe, the *Vesta,* will enter Mars's orbit. This second craft, a 770-pound (350-kilogram) Soviet orbiter, will fire two lancelike sensors into the Martian ground. The *Vesta* will also release a French Space Agency balloon in early 1996 that will descend through the thin air of Mars to collect soil samples. This balloon will not be anchored to one spot like the Viking landers or the *Vesta*'s sensors. It will be capable of covering 300 miles (500 kilometers) per day, and it will move over the entire planet. Its builders expect that it will roam over some 3,000 miles (5,000 kilometers) of Mars.

The United States, like France, will also be cooperating in the Vesta mission. NASA will mount an antenna on the *Mars Observer* that will relay signals from the *Vesta*'s balloon experiment to Earth. The Soviets in return will be placing a NASA-sponsored instrument on one of their future Mars-bound craft.

THE MARS-SAMPLE RETURN MISSION

What lies beyond these two missions? The Soviet Union hopes to land a surface rover on Mars two years after Vesta. This vehicle, carrying two burrowing devices called moles, will collect samples from as deep as 100 feet (30 meters). It also will conduct biological experiments and search for Martian fossils at various sites around Mars.

The Mars-Sample Return Mission may follow the surface rover mission. Both the United States and the Soviet Union have made on-again, off-again plans for this project for years. The mission's purpose will be simple: send an automated probe to Mars to collect soil and rock and bring them back to Earth. The goal may sound simple, but the execution will be both difficult and expensive. The two countries have recently begun serious talks about a cooperative Mars-Sample Return Mission in hopes of eliminating some of the problems facing such a project.

The mission will require at a bare minimum an orbital vehicle, a lander, and a surface rover. Upon reaching Mars, the orbiter will launch the lander toward the surface below (Figure 19). This automated landing will be one of the trickiest parts of the whole mission because the lander must make the descent and touchdown on its own. Ground Control will be twenty minutes away by radio, and by the time the controllers find out about a problem, either the lander will have solved it or the mission will have ended in a crash landing. NASA will make its greatest contribution to the project by building and controlling the lander.

NASA has not only the better technology but also the experience of two previous successful landings on Mars.

Upon engine cutoff, the lander will release the surface rover (Figure 20). This rover will be a four-wheeled robot looking very much like the lunar buggies used by the Apollo astronauts. It will immediately collect soil samples after its release and will deposit them inside the lander. These samples will help ensure the success of the mission even if later the rover should break down or the lander has to lift off suddenly. The Soviet Union's major role in the project will be building and guiding the rover. The Soviets, between 1969 and 1971, sent several such surface rovers to the Moon, and all those vehicles worked superbly, supplying as much information about the Moon as the Apollo missions did.

The rover will move from one preselected site to another for the next several weeks as it collects samples. It eventually will return to the lander and will load the samples aboard. The rover then will retreat out of range of the lander's rocket exhaust since it will remain on Mars for further work. The lander will lift off and dock with the orbiter, which will blast out of orbit for the return to Earth. When it reaches Earth, the orbiter will either jettison the samples for retrieval by a space shuttle crew, or it will actually land, depending much as did the Apollo capsules, upon a heat shield and parachute to make the descent through the atmosphere. The Martian samples will give planetary scientists their first opportunity to see what Mars rocks are really like.

PUTTING HUMANS ON MARS

All the above missions have one thing in common. They depend upon automated spacecraft to collect

data and samples from Mars. Will humans follow the machines to Mars? The United States and the Soviet Union are both making plans for such a mission sometime in the next century. Sending humans to Mars may even become a joint venture of the two countries.

Scientists such as Wernher von Braun, a designer of the German V-2 rocket and one of the architects of the U.S. Apollo program, as far back as the early 1950s proposed sending a human crew to Mars. One of the first NASA plans was to land astronauts first on the Moon and then on Mars. In this plan the 1960s would have seen the first space station orbiting the Earth. This station would have been the launch point for crewed missions to both the Moon and Mars. NASA finally decided that this plan was too expensive and complex, and the agency opted instead for the Apollo program that sent astronauts directly from the Earth to the Moon.

NASA, looking for a follow-up to the successful Apollo program, once more made plans for the crewed Mars mission to be accomplished by the 1980s. The new plan called for a reusable spaceship, the space shuttle, which would be used to build a space station. The station would again be the orbital base from which ships would go out to Mars. The plan ran into financial problems when Congress cut NASA's operating

Figure 19. Top: artist's illustration showing touchdown on Mars of a sample-return vehicle. Figure 20. Bottom: a Mars sample-return mission would use an automated rover to collect samples.

budget in the early 1970s. The result of the new budget was a drastic redesign of the shuttle, and the elimination of both the space station and the Mars mission.

NASA in the 1990s again has plans for a space station, and it is also once more talking about a crewed Mars mission. Is a space station really essential for a trip to Mars? Yes, it is, even though NASA managed to send twenty-seven astronauts to the Moon and bring them back without such a station. To send three men to the Moon with all the supplies to keep them alive for just a few days required the huge *Saturn 5* booster. These boosters are no longer built, and even the giant launchpads needed for them have all been ripped out and destroyed. NASA could rebuild the pads and *Saturn 5* boosters for less than the cost of a space station, but even if the agency did, the *Saturn 5* could not launch a Mars ship. The trip to Mars will take two to three years, and the Mars craft will have to be many times larger than an Apollo capsule to carry the supplies and fuel for so long a journey. Such a craft would be far too large and heavy for even the mightiest rocket to carry into space. The ship, therefore, cannot be launched in one piece from Earth, so it must be built in Earth orbit. The people who build it must have some place to live—the space station.

A failure on Congress's part to continue funding the space station project, as happened in the seventies, could kill it. A cooperative U.S.-U.S.S.R. Mars mission, however, could still proceed even if the NASA station does not materialize. The Soviets in the late 1980s launched the first section of what is to be a large space station called *Mir,* which means "peace" in Russian. A joint U.S.-U.S.S.R. mission would still have its orbital launchpad even without a U.S. space station.

The existence of the Soviet station is not the only reason for such a cooperative Mars mission. Such a crewed Mars mission will cost at least as much as the entire Apollo program, 60 billion dollars (some estimates run as high as 300 billion dollars), and the two countries could halve that by sharing expenses. Both countries, as with a Mars-Sample Return Mission, would have strengths the other lacks. The United States would have the superior technology and the lessons learned from Apollo. The Soviet Union would have the most experience with the physical and psychological problems that humans will face on such a long space flight. Dozens of cosmonauts have spent months at a time in space on board the small orbital research station *Salyut*.

A DIFFICULT AND
DANGEROUS MISSION

The problems facing even a joint mission will still be great, and one of the greatest will be ensuring the welfare and safety of the crew. A few people will spend two to three years together, first in a small ship and then in a tiny, Martian base. Some Soviet cosmonauts on long-term missions in the *Salyut* station reached the point where they would not even speak to one another, while one pair actually started a fistfight. Such friction will be a real danger to the crew of the Mars mission, so they will have to be chosen carefully.

Weightlessness is another potential problem. The crew will be weightless except when on Mars for most of their years-long voyage, and this condition could pose as much danger to them as any challenge they meet on Mars. The Soviets have had cosmonauts in space for as much as a year at a time. These men have suffered bone and muscle loss and experienced circulatory problems from their prolonged weightlessness. The only answer for the Mars crew may be exercise, hours of exercise every day. At Mars, those aboard the ship will need to rotate with those on the planet's surface, so no one spends too many consecutive months in weightlessness.

Radiation is another hazard the crew of a Mars ship may face, particularly from solar flares. Regions of the sun periodically brighten and shoot out large bursts of radiation such as X rays. These solar flares generally do little harm to Earth outside of disrupting radio and TV signals. The Earth's magnetic field and atmosphere prevent most of the flare's radiation from reaching the surface. The crew of a Mars ship caught in space during one of these flares would have no such protection. The ship will therefore need a thickly shielded section at its center that will act as a storm cellar for the crew in the event that a solar flare should erupt during the journey.

Both American and Soviet planners generally agree that the shortest trip time to and from Mars would reduce the dangers from interpersonal friction, from weightlessness, and from radiation. Few of them, however, favor a fast journey to the fourth planet because the shortest possible trip would require too much fuel, particularly if no way is found to manufacture more once at Mars. The fast trip would also provide too little time for the crew to explore Mars. The ship will probably leave when Earth and Mars are making their closest approach to each other. The expedition will have to remain at Mars until the two planets again move close to each other. This fuel-conserving trip will take two and one-half years (Figure 21). The trip to Mars will last six months. The crew will then spend nineteen months on Mars and take another six months to return to Earth.

The crew will occupy the long journey to Mars by conducting experiments and making observations as they approach the fourth planet. They will also play games, exercise, and respect each other's privacy.

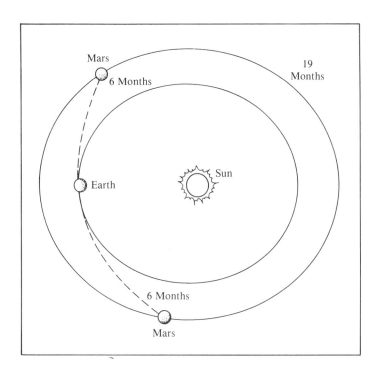

*Figure 21. The most fuel-efficient course to Mars has
a ship taking six months to reach the fourth planet.
The astronauts would then spend nineteen months
exploring Mars and take another six months
to make the return flight to Earth.*

Upon reaching Mars the ship will remain in orbit while
part of the crew enters a landing craft and descends to
the surface. The landing party will dig an underground shelter since the atmosphere of Mars offers no
protection from solar radiation, particularly flares. The
ground-based crew will spend the next several months
setting up instruments and collecting samples. Some
of them will also make field trips to nearby areas. The
members of the crew remaining aboard the mother

93

ship in orbit will also be busy monitoring their own scientific experiments. They will probably visit Phobos and perhaps even Deimos.

A MARS BASE

Is such a mission really worth the expense and danger involved? American and Soviet planners believe so since humans are far more versatile and adaptable than machines, but to make such a mission truly worthwhile, future plans call for a permanent base on Mars. The first explorers on Mars, no matter how well trained, will not be able to examine even a small fraction of the planet, and a permanent base will mean continuing study of the red planet.

Is such a base possible? Many planetary scientists think so, although the base's existence depends on what is learned about Mars in the next few years. Robot cargo ships would supply this base with food, air, fuel, and construction material, but if the base personnel can find ice or water nearby, the cost of this supply run will be reduced. Martian water would eliminate the need to ship one of the most essential as well as bulkiest of human necessities across interplanetary space. It would also allow the base to grow its own vegetables, although fertilizer would probably have to be sent from Earth since Mars has little nitrogen in its air or soil. Water would give the base the raw materials to make its own fuel for shuttles with which to meet incoming passenger and supply ships.

Other countries may set up their own research stations on Mars, much as has been done in Antarctica The scientists at these stations would continue studying the processes that formed Mars, and they would also continue searching for signs of past or present Martian life. These scientists may even bring their families with them since they would probably be away from Earth for several years. They may even come to call Mars home.

The real Mars has and continues to be important in the study of the planets of the solar system, particularly in the understanding of the Earth. Yet Mars has also played another role, a fictional role. With the publication of his book *Mars*, in 1896, Percival Lowell made Mars a desirable piece of fictional real estate. No other body in the solar system, including the Moon, has been the setting for more science fiction novels and stories than Mars, and just as the picture of the real Mars has changed throughout the twentieth century, so has the fictional Mars.

8

THE FICTIONAL MARS

The planet Mars is a real place, but it is also a fictitious place, a fantastical playground for the imagination. The fictional Mars sometimes corresponds exactly with the real Mars, and sometimes it does not, but the planet has furnished the setting for everything from satire to adventure. Martian novels range from outright fantasies to well-grounded scientific speculations. They provide sheer entertainment as well as insights into human psychology and social behavior.

The earliest novels dealing with Mars are heavy on message and short on story. Such novels as *Across the Zodiac** (1880) by Percy Greg and *Mr. Stranger's Sealed Packet* (1889) by Hugh MacColl drop their protagonists into Martian society. Both books are utopian novels in which the author uses Mars merely as a

---

* *Note: In this chapter, titles of books are italicized, while those of short stories are placed in quotation marks.*

conveniently isolated location to place his version of the perfect human society. Either could just as easily have been set on a remote island in the Pacific Ocean.

PLANET OF ADVENTURE

After the turn of the century, Mars as utopia lost favor with readers. An occasional novel such as C. S. Lewis's *Out of the Silent Planet* (1938) makes use of the Martian utopia, but with the publication of Percival Lowell's book *Mars* (1896), turn-of-the-century readers demanded the same romantic elements in their Martian fiction. They wanted an ancient world, dying as the last of its water disappears. They wanted intelligent Martians engaged in a heroic struggle against the encroaching deserts. They wanted giant canals carrying much needed water from poles to farmlands. With Edgar Rice Burroughs they got the ancient Mars, the heroic Martians, and the giant canals, although not quite as Lowell had envisioned them.

Burroughs's Mars is an exotic locale, full of old, half-understood mysteries, where both evil and good battle in the ruins of their former glories. No one can call these novels slow-moving. Beginning with *A Princess of Mars* in 1917, the creator of Tarzan launched his Earth hero, John Carter, into a world full of nonstop action, friendly aliens, villainous humans, and strange beasts. All this is set against the backdrop of a dying world, maintained by oxygen from giant manufacturing plants and water pumped from the polar caps through immense canals.

The civilization John Carter finds on Mars is an odd mix. Battles are waged with swords, while combatants travel in antigravity ships. In Burroughs's Mars novels, Lowell's race of master engineers is long dead, and Burroughs's Martians have long since begun to forget their science. The pumping stations and air plants are leftovers from a distant past, using a technology that no living Martian really understands. The average Burroughs Martian is more at home with a sword than with a physics text.

Burroughs's eleven novels about Mars were immensely popular during his lifetime and are still in print today, probably being read by more people than when the author was alive. Burroughs's Martian novels also gave rise to a long line of successors. During his lifetime, imitators such as Otis Adelbert Kline wrote novels such as *The Swordsman of Mars* (1933) and *The Outlaws of Mars* (1933) that use the same dying planet with its mix of ancient technologies and medieval weaponry.

Other writers trying to avoid repeating Burroughs too closely made their cultures more exotic. The people and places are very much like those found in adventure novels set in the Far East. There is more of Rudyard Kipling and Talbot Mundy's India in these Martian novels than of Percival Lowell's Mars. As with Kipling and Mundy's Indians, the Martians of "Shambleau" (1933) by C. L. Moore and *The Sword of Rhiannon* (1953) by Leigh Brackett are the inheritors of very old traditions and are too mysterious for the average Earth man or woman to understand. Theirs is a culture of half-hidden secrets, governed by decadent rulers and terrorized by ancient cults. Such stories are great fun, and many of them are still in print even though the Mars they portray has been scholarly dust for decades. Their very scientific falseness seems to attract some writers, for authors such as Lin Carter were writing about this exotic Mars well into the 1980s.

In all of these novels inspired by Burroughs, at least some of the native Martians are human. The writer sometimes explains the presence of humans on Mars by the device of a long-ago interplanetary empire, as in Wallace West's *Lords of Atlantis* (1960). More often, no explanation is given. Obviously human Martians are an easy way to give the Earth hero someone to fight beside, rescue, and marry. The Martians' humanness can be more essential to the plot in some stories. In Roger Zelazny's "A Rose for Ecclesiastes" (1963), the terrestrial protagonist finds that without him Mars is doomed since all Martian males are sterile.

AT WAR WITH MARS

Fictional Martians are not always human. One early story containing nonhuman Martians is Stanley G. Weinbaum's "A Martian Odyssey" (1934). As the humans follow their birdlike guide, Tweel, they meet one nonhuman society after another. Weinbaum wanted his Martians to be natives of another planet, not just humans in fancy dress. Twell, although clearly a bird, does not fly. Instead, he leaps though the air, landing like a living arrow by impaling the ground with his sharp beak. Weinbaum attempts to make the actions of these Martians both alien and incomprehensible to the human protagonists and readers.

Among the earliest and most famous Martians of all were those of H. G. Wells's *War of the Worlds* (1898). Wells's Martians were not remotely human-shaped, being octopoidlike creatures who thrived on human blood. Psychologically, however, these Martians are very humanlike, particularly in their motives for invading Earth. Wells, like almost every other writer, made his Mars a dying world. His Martians decide to conquer the Earth to escape their impoverished planet.

Wells was not really interested in Mars or Martians. His Martians and his interplanetary war became the means by which he discussed the failings of hu-

*Figure 22. The Martian death machines
in the film* War of the Worlds.

man society. Yet it is not Wells's preaching that readers generally remember from *War of the Worlds*. It is
the Martian war machines striding (Figure 22) across
a devastated Earth. It is an image reinforced by the
1953 movie and by the recent TV series (although in
the series, the invaders are just aliens, no longer Martians).

War of the Worlds inspired any number of novels
that take place either before, during, or after the Martian invasion. Garrett P. Serviss's *Edison's Conquest of
Mars* (1898) sends Thomas Edison to Mars to teach
the Martians a lesson, while Christopher Priest's *The
Space Machine* (1976) has a British salesman and his
girlfriend marooned on Mars just prior to the inva-

sion. In *Sherlock Holmes's War of the Worlds* (1975), Manly Wade Wellman and Wade Wellman enlist the aid of Sir Arthur Conan Doyle's famous detective in *War of the Worlds*. Another of Doyle's characters, Professor Challenger of *The Lost World* fame, also lends a hand. One of the most unusual spinoffs of Wells's novel is *The Alternate Martians* (1965) by A. Bertram Chandler. In this novel a spaceship crew finds itself on an alternate Mars that combines elements of the Mars of both Wells and Burroughs. A group of ex-slaves led by Bill Carter opposes huge octopoid Martians who drink human blood.

Wells was not the last writer to picture Martians as warlike. In C. M. Kornbluth's "The Silly Season" (1950), the Martians launch their invasion during the summer so their activities are hidden among that season's crackpot stories. Such silly season stories fill newspapers and TV news programs. In *Nomad* (1950) by George O. Smith, Earth and Mars are locked in an interplanetary war that ends only with the intervention of a planet from outside the solar system. Earth loses such a war to Mars in Poul Anderson's *War of Two Worlds* (1959), and the protagonist, a former soldier, comes home to an occupied Earth. Wallace West in *The Bird of Time* (1959) has his Martians using trickery and telepathy to try and conquer the Earth (to be fair the Earth also is attempting to conquer Mars). Finally in "How the Heroes Die" (1966), Larry Niven has a scientific outpost on Mars wiped out by underground-dwelling Martians. Niven's story is noteworthy as being the first story set on the Mars revealed by NASA's 1965 *Mariner 4* spacecraft.

HUMANS AND MARTIANS

Not all fictional Martians are warlike: sometimes they are the victims and the people of Earth the invaders and conquerors. In Ray Bradbury's classic *The Martian Chronicles* (1950), the people of Earth come and, despite every effort on the part of the native Martians, overrun and settle Mars. Bradbury's Martians die off during this human invasion. Bradbury, like Wells, is not interested in the reality of Mars—then or now. His Mars is very earthlike, and humans have no difficulty in relocating not only themselves, but their entire culture. Mars is a means by which the author can show the reader something about human nature. Bradbury finds Mars a convenient setting for a story that parallels the effects of European colonialism on Asia, Africa, and the Americas. It is no accident that this Mars looks and resembles a rather exotic U.S. Midwest. One chapter even has the Martians attempting to fool an Earth expedition into thinking they have returned to its members' midwestern hometown. (See Figure 23.)

Bradbury does not make the mistake of making his Martians simply noble victims of human greed. They are as complicated and flawed as his humans, and most of them are as unwilling to accept and understand humans as the humans are to tolerate them. The humans of *The Martian Chronicles* are also no mere cardboard villains. Their attraction for their new home is often mixed with their guilt over the death of the native Martians. This guilt begins disappearing only after the Earth destroys itself in nuclear war, and the settlers realize that, with the death of their home planet, they are now the Martians.

In some Martian fiction, neither Martians nor humans fight one another. P. Schuyler Miller's "The Cave" (1943), Poul Anderson's *Shield* (1963), and Robert A. Heinlein's *Red Planet* (1949) and *Stranger in a Strange Land* (1961) present Martians who belong to a wise, elderly race and who are often willing to help out their younger and less sophisticated terrestrial neighbors. The peaceful Martians sometimes

Figure 23. A Martian in the television miniseries of Ray Bradbury's The Martian Chronicles.

actually come to Earth. They are here to keep a close watch on their dangerous neighbors in Edgar Pangborn's *A Mirror for Observers* (1954), while in Ian Watson's *The Martian Inca* (1977) Martians come to teach humans a new philosophy.

PRIMITIVE MARS

The inhabitants of the fictional Mars are not always technologically advanced. Some are even primitive. Lester del Ray in *Marooned on Mars* (1952) has the first humans on Mars stumble upon the barbaric remnants of a once advanced culture, while *The Sands of Mars* (1951) by Arthur C. Clarke and *Outpost Mars* (1952) by C. M. Kornbluth and Judith Merrill (writing as Cyril Judd) show Martians stuck in their Stone Age. These three novels show a much more hostile Mars than those of earlier science fiction writers. The Martian data, collected by astronomers of the early 1950s, showed clearly that only a primitive, hunting-and-gathering society was likely to evolve in conditions so harsh—except in light of present-day knowledge. The members of such a society, however, do not need to be savages. Philip K. Dick's *Martian Time-Slip* (1964) gives the Martians a culture very similar to the Australian aborigines'. Although the human settlers considered them inferior, the Martians prove to be the ones who have the insight and knowledge to help several troubled colonists.

Until 1950, science fiction writers generally ignored the most pessimistic findings about Mars. That was easy enough since astronomers were far from agreeing about conditions on the fourth planet. Many instruments of that period were not as reliable as those of later decades. In the 1950s the instrumentation became better and the data more accurate. Mars was not a friendly place for terrestrial life-forms. It might not even be a healthy place for any form of life. These new findings about the red planet began to appear in stories set on Mars.

H. Beam Piper's "Omnilingual" (1957) and Samuel R. Delany's "High Weir" (1968) present a Mars that is no longer habitable. All the Martians are long dead, and human scientists wander wonderingly through the ruins of cities, trying to learn about the dead aliens. Mars is not left entirely lifeless in such stories. There is still plant life, although even mere vegetation (at least if it's Martian) is not always harmless. Kenneth F. Gantz's *Not in Solitude* (1959) has a Mars where only plants survive, but Gantz's plants turn out to be a deadly intelligent force. His terrestrial spaceship barely escapes this chlorophyll menace.

FRONTIER WORLD

The 1950s and 1960s saw the emergence of a new type of Martian story, the pseudodocumentary, which is so scrupulously researched as to appear to be an actual record of real events. Some pseudodocumentaries barely reach Mars, ending with the landing on that planet. They find their drama not on Mars but either in the struggle of getting the expedition launched, as in Allen Drury's *The Throne of Saturn* (1971) and Jack Bickham's *Day Seven* (1988), or in the difficulty of the actual flight, as in Gordon R. Dickson's *The Far Call* (1978). Generally conflict in such Mars stories arises from the struggle of humans with the harsh Martian environment. Arthur C. Clarke's *The Sands of Mars* (1951), E. C. Tubb's *Alien Dust* (1955), Theodore Sturgeon's "The Man Who Lost the Sea" (1959), and Frederik Pohl's *Man Plus* (1976) are as realistic and scientifically accurate as the writers could make them. In each, the protagonists grapple with conditions hostile not just to human life, but to all life. The struggle with Mars is sometimes won by finding water offplanet as the colonists do in Isaac Asimov's "The Martian Way" (1952). Sometimes it is won by physically adapting, such as developing larger lung capacity as in John Brunner's *Born under Mars* (1967).

The Mars of the pseudodocumentary tends to be a frontier not unlike the American Southwest or the Outback of Australia. It is a planet dotted with small settlements that have few luxuries. When the writer becomes lazy, such stories are little more than Westerns set on Mars as happens in Jerry Sohl's *The Mars*

Monopoly (1956) and Frank Belknap Long's *Space Station #1* (1957).

As with any frontier, colonies are established for a variety of reasons. The fictional Mars, like Georgia and Australia in Earth's past, becomes the perfect place to dump Earth's criminals. Lester del Rey (writing as Erik van Lihn) creates a Devil's Island out of Mars in *Police Your Planet* (1956), while D. G. Compton in *Farewell, Earth's Bliss* (1966) shows the despair of those exiled to such penal colonies. Jerry E. Pournelle's *Birth of Fire* (1976) and Lester del Rey's *Badge of Infamy* (1957) follow the successful revolts of such prison settlements from Earth control. A. Bertram Chandler brings everything full circle. His *The Bitter Pill* (1974) describes a Martian penal colony called Botany Bay most of whose settlers are Australian political prisoners.

Mars also functions as the final refuge for humanity when some natural or human-made disaster destroys Earth. J. T. McIntosh sends a select group of people to Mars after solar flares make Earth uninhabitable in *One in Three Hundred* (1954), while in Lan Wright's *The Last Hope of Earth* (1964), the Martian colony provides a sanctuary for people escaping an Earth whose oceans are smothering under an uncontrollable weed. Poul Anderson has two groups fight for the right to settle their refugees on Mars in *Twilight World* (1961).

Martian colonists, who have been cut off from the home world for centuries, sometimes return to Earth. Lester del Rey's colonist in *The Eleventh Commandment* (1962) finds an appallingly overcrowded Earth run by an oppressive religion. A returning human finds a decadent society, existing without purpose, in Algis Budrys's *The Amsirs and the Iron Thorn* (1967). Such stories, as with those of Wells and Bradbury, are more concerned with examining human failings than with exploring Mars.

106

When Mars isn't being a human prison or refugee camp, it is a base for aliens from worlds beyond the solar system. These interstellar visitors leave a mysterious object on the fourth planet in *The Martian Sphinx* (1965) by John Brunner (writing as Keith Woodcott), and in *The Brass Dragon* (1968) by Marion Zimmer Bradley, they use Mars as an advance base for a planned attack on Earth.

MARS AND THE MOVIES

Science-fiction movies have not ignored Mars, either. These cinematic efforts range from such special-effects spectaculars as *War of the Worlds* (1953), in which Gene Barry fights a hopeless battle against the invading Martians, who ultimately died from our bacteria, to such low-budget disasters as *Mission Mars* (1968), in which Darren McGavin and Nick Adams fly their beer-can-shaped spaceship to a crash-landing on Mars.

One of the earliest films to use Mars and Martians is *A Message from Mars* (1913). Based on a stage play, it has a Martian sent to Earth to reform a particularly nasty old man. The Martian succeeds after much effort in much the same way as the three spirits do with Scrooge in "A Christmas Carol." Another attempt to send the movie audience a message is *Rocketship X-M* (1950). Lloyd Bridges and company land on Mars only to find it a radioactive wasteland (Figure 24). They are attacked by the Martians, who have been blinded as the result of nuclear war (originally, the script called for a landing on the Moon, but the release of *Destination Moon* the same year demanded a quick course change for both script and ship).

As with many science fiction stories and novels, movie Martians tend to be hostile and dangerous. In such films as *Flight to Mars* (1951) and *The Angry Red Planet* (1960), human explorers step out of their

107

Figure 24. A scene from the film Rocketship X-M. *How accurate is the portrayal of the Martian surface?*

ships right into trouble with the Martians. Often the red-planet denizens are out to conquer the Earth, whether from underground as in *Invaders from Mars* (1953) or from the distant past as in *Five Million Years to Earth* (1967). Only *Conquest of Space* (1954) portrays the trip to Mars, and Mars itself, realistically. Based on *The Mars Project* by Wernher von Braun, the film is as scientifically accurate as possible for the time. The storyline, unfortunately, is as bad as the science is good. (See Figure 25.)

108

A more entertaining—although far less accurate—film, is *Robinson Crusoe on Mars* (1964). Here the alien menace is from another planet and uses human slaves to mine Mars for valuable minerals. The stranded Earth hero helps dispose of these slave drivers after befriending an escaped slave.

One of the oddest Martian movies is the science fiction musical *Just Imagine* (1930), in which two early twentieth-century humans are revived in time to travel to Mars. A big-budget film for its time, its spaceship sequences would be used later in the Flash Gordon serials.

Almost as odd are two 1970s films, *The Astronaut* (1971) and *Capricorn One* (1977) both involving NASA hoaxes. *The Astronaut* is the first human to reach Mars only to die. So that no one will learn the truth, NASA substitutes a double for the dead man. The double, however, is unable to fool the dead man's wife. In *Capricorn One*, NASA lacks the funds to send three astronauts to Mars, so it fakes the launch and mission. The deception fails when one of the astronauts successfully escapes.

THE LIVING MARS

No matter what a writer or screenwriter's reasons for using Mars in story or film, he or she almost always shows us a Mars with life on it. Even the failure in 1976 of NASA's Viking mission to find any trace of life on Mars has not resulted in a lifeless fictional Mars. Martian life is merely single-celled plants hiding in crevices in William Walling's "Nix Olympica" (1974), while in John Varley's "In the Halls of the Martian King" (1977), such life survives as spores beneath the surface, waiting for the first drops of water. Bob Buckley's "Encounter under Tharsis" (1974) and Frederik Pohl's

109

Figure 25. Scenes from three films:
top left, Flight to Mars,
bottom left, The Angry Red Planet,
above, Invaders from Mars

recent *The Day the Martians Came* (1988) have intelligent Martians surviving underground.

Since the beginning of astronomical observation of Mars, scientists and nonscientists alike have hoped the fourth planet had life. There is something in us humans that hungers to know we are not alone, that we are not the only life in the universe. Most likely that other life exists on planets orbiting other stars, but we cannot reach those planets yet and will not be able to for a long time to come.

We keep hoping that Mars, which we *have* reached, is, like Earth, a home for life in our own solar system. Over the past 200 years, Martian life has become one of our myths, and no matter how harsh the conditions on Mars, we will not give up hoping to find such life until the last grain of sand has been examined and the planet explored to its core.

The real Mars we have discovered through our interplanetary probes does not even remotely resemble the Mars of Percival Lowell and Edgar Rice Burroughs, yet it is as exotic as their Mars. It is a small world, but it is populated by giants, and it is a world that has as much in common with our Earth as did that ancient, dying world created by turn-of-the-century astronomy.

Appendix 1
THE PHYSICAL
CHARACTERISTICS
OF MARS AND EARTH

	Mars	Earth
mean distance from Sun	141.3 million miles (227.9 million kilometers)	92.9 million miles (149.6 million kilometers)
length of year	687 days	365 days
length of day	24 hours 37 minutes	23 hours 56 minutes
diameter	4,200 miles (6,800 kilometers)	7,920 miles (12,760 kilometers)
surface gravity (percent of Earth normal)	0.38	1.00
escape velocity	3.2 miles per second (5.1 kilometers per second)	7.0 miles per second (11.2 kilometers per second)
mean surface temperature	−9 degrees Fahrenheit (−23 degrees Celsius)	72 degrees Fahrenheit (22 degrees Celsius)
atmospheric pressure on surface	6.1 millibars	1 bar
moons	2	1

Appendix 2
THE ATMOSPHERE OF MARS AND EARTH

	Mars	Earth
carbon dioxide	96.5%	0.03%
nitrogen	1.8%	78.1%
argon	1.5%	0.9%
oxygen	0.1%	20.9%
water	0.06%	1.6%

Appendix 3
THE PHYSICAL CHARACTERISTICS OF PHOBOS, DEIMOS, AND THE MOON

	Phobos	Deimos	Moon
distance from planet	5,830 miles (9,380 kilometers)	14,600 miles (23,500 kilometers)	238,300 miles (384,400 kilometers)
period of revolution	7.6 hours	30 hours	27 days
dimensions	16.7 miles (25 kilometers), long axis	7.5 miles (13 kilometers), long axis	2,160 miles (3,480 kilometers), diameter
escape velocity	25.7 feet per second (7.8 meters per second)	15.5 feet per second (4.7 meters per second)	1.5 miles per second (2.4 kilometers per second)
reflectivity (percent of lunar normal)	0.5	0.5	1.0

Appendix 4
MISSIONS TO MARS

Mars 1*
U.S.S.R.
Launched: November 1, 1962; arrived: ———
Ground control lost radio contact on June 21, 1963.

Mariner 4
U.S.
Launched: November 8, 1964; arrived: July 15, 1965
Took 22 photographs of the Martian surface and measured
   the density and composition of the atmosphere.

Zond 2
U.S.S.R.
Launched: November 30, 1964; arrived: August 2, 1965
Ceased radio transmissions when it reached Mars.

Mariner 6
U.S.
Launched: February 24, 1969; arrived: July 31, 1969
Orbited Mars above the equator.

Mariner 7
U.S.
Launched: March 27, 1969; arrived: August 5, 1969
Orbited above Mars's southern hemisphere.

Took over 200 photographs of Mars, found no ozone in
   atmosphere, and detected frozen carbon dioxide at the
   south pole, as well as signs of water and wind erosion
   on the surface.

Mariner 8
U.S.
Launched: May 8, 1971; arrived: ———
Crashed in the Atlantic upon lift-off.

Mars 2
U.S.S.R.
Launched: May 19, 1971; arrived: November 27, 1971
Deployed landing capsule that crashed on surface. Orbited
   Mars for three months, measuring surface tempera-
   tures, water vapor and other gases in atmosphere, and
   photographing surface.

Mars 3

　U.S.S.R.

　Launched: May 28, 1971; arrived: December 2, 1971

　Landed capsule on surface whose transmissions ceased after
　　twenty seconds. Orbited Mars for three months survey-
　　ing surface. Determined the amounts of uranium and
　　thorium in the Martian soil to be similar to that found
　　on Earth.

Mariner 9

　U.S.

　Launched: May 30, 1971; arrived: November 13, 1971

　Spent almost a year orbiting planet, taking over 7,000 pho-
　　tographs that covered 90 percent of the Martian surface.
　　Also took first pictures of the two moons of Mars.

Mars 4

　U.S.S.R.

　Launched: July 21, 1973; arrived: February 1974

　Failed to take up orbit around Mars.

Mars 5

　U.S.S.R.

　Launched: July 25, 1973; arrived: February 1974

　Died in orbit after two weeks, but may have detected a weak
　　magnetic field around the planet.

Mars 6

　U.S.S.R.

　Launched: August 5, 1973; arrived: March 1974

　Deployed capsule that crashed attempting landing.

Mars 7

　U.S.S.R.

　Launched: August 9, 1973; arrived: March 1974

　Deployed landing capsule that missed the planet.

Viking 1

　U.S.

　Launched: August 20, 1975; arrived: June 19, 1976

　Deployed lander that touched down on July 20, 1976, and
　　that conducted biological experiments, as well as soil
　　and atmospheric analysis. Orbiter photographed sur-
　　face.

Viking 2

　U.S.

　Launched: September 9, 1975; arrived: August 7, 1976

Deployed lander that touched down on September 3, 1976, 3,100 miles (5,000 kilometers) from lander 1. Orbiter photographed surface.

Through summer of 1980, landers sent 3 million weather reports, while orbiters sent back over 50,000 photographs, covering 97 percent of the surface as well as both moons. The last Viking transmission was from lander *1* on November 5, 1982, and scientists are still processing Viking data in the 1990s.

Phobos 1
U.S.S.R.
Launched: July 7, 1988; arrived: ———
Ground control lost contact on September 14, 1988.

Phobos 2
U.S.S.R.
Launched: July 12, 1988; arrived: February 5, 1989
Orbited Mars for six weeks, photographing the moon Phobos as well as searching its surface for traces of water. Failed to discover if Mars does or does not have a weak magnetic field. Died in orbit before deploying capsule for landing on Phobos.

Mars Observer
U.S.
Launched: 1992; will arrive: 1993
Will take up a polar orbit and search for a Martian magnetic field and subsurface ice and water, as well as measure surface elevation.

Vesta
U.S.S.R.
Launched: 1994; will arrive: 1995
Will release two probes and a French-built balloon to analyze soil and atmosphere.

---

* Note: The Soviet Union attempted to launch two probes to Mars in October 1960. They were both destroyed when the rockets carrying them exploded. The second accident happened while the space vehicle was still on the ground and killed a number of people.

Glossary

Caldera. A bowl-shaped depression at the summit of a volcano caused when the volcanic cone collapses.

Canali. Natural channels that supposedly crossed the Martian surface. Some nineteenth- and early-twentieth-century astronomers believed they were artificial waterways or canals, but they were actually optical illusions.

Greenhouse effect. An atmospheric process in which carbon dioxide and water vapor trap heat radiated from the Earth's surface and prevent that heat from escaping into space.

Magma. Hot, melted rock, lying beneath the planetary crust.

Sapping. The undercutting of a cliff by groundwater or ice. The water or ice carries off small bits of the cliff base until the rock wall gives way in a landslide.

Shield volcano. A volcano such as Olympus Mons on Mars and Mauna Loa on Earth whose various eruptions of lava build up a dome that looks like a circular shield.

Tectonic plates. Sections of the Earth's crust that float on the magma beneath.

For Further Reading
and Viewing

NONFICTION

Baugher, Joseph F. *The Space-Age Solar System*. New York: Wiley, 1988.

Beatty, J. Kelly. "The Amazing Olympus Mons." *Sky & Telescope*, November 1982.

Carroll, Michael. "The Changing Face of Mars." *Astonomy*, March 1987.

Collins, Michael. "Mission to Mars." *National Geographic*, November 1988.

Cooper, H. *The Search for Life on Mars*. New York: Holt, Rinehart & Winston, 1980.

Cordell, Bruce. "Mars, Earth, and Ice." *Sky & Telescope*, July 1986.

Eberhart, Jonathan. "Phobos: Mission to a Martian Potato." *Science News*, June 18, 1988.

Goldman, Stuart J. "The Legacy of Phobos 2." *Sky & Telescope*, February 1990.

Haberle, Robert M. "The Climate of Mars." *Scientific American*, May 1986.

Ley, Willy. *Watchers of the Skies: An Informal History of Astronomy from Babylon to the Space Age*. New York: Viking, 1963.

Schultz, Peter H. "Polar Wandering on Mars." *Scientific American*, December 1985.

Tennesen, Michael. "Mars: Remembrance of Life Past." *Discover.* July 1989.

FICTION

Brackett, Leigh. *The Sword of Rhiannon.* New York: Ace, 1953.

Bradbury, Ray. *The Martian Chronicles.* New York: Doubleday, 1950.

Burroughs, Edgar Rice. *The Gods of Mars.* Chicago: McClurg, 1918.

———. *A Princess of Mars.* Chicago: McClurg, 1917.

———. *The Warlord of Mars.* Chicago: McClurg, 1919.

Clarke, Arthur C. *The Sands of Mars.* London: Sidgwick & Jackson, 1951.

Delany, Samuel R. "High Weir." *Worlds of If,* October 1968.

Dickson, Gordon R. *The Far Call.* New York: Dial, 1978.

Farren, Mick. *Mars—The Red Planet.* New York: Del Rey, 1990.

Heinlein. Robert A. *Red Planet.* New York: Scribner's, 1949; complete text, New York: Del Rey, 1990.

———. *Stranger in a Strange Land.* New York: Putnam's, 1961; complete text, New York: Putnam's, 1991.

Hipolito, John, and Willis E. McNelly, ed. *Mars, We Love You: Tales of Mars, Men, and Martians.* New York: Doubleday, 1971.

Lewis, C. S. *Out of the Silent Planet.* London: Lane, 1938.

Niven, Larry. "How the Heroes Die." *Galaxy,* October 1966.

Pohl, Frederik. *The Day the Martians Came.* New York: St. Martin's, 1988.

Pournelle, Jerry E. *Birth of Fire.* Toronto: Laser, 1976; revised, New York: Pocket Books, 1978.

Robinson, Kim Stanley. *Green Mars.* New York: Tor, 1988.

Steele, Allen M. "Red Planet Blues." *Isaac Asimov's Science Fiction Magazine,* September 1989.

Wells, H. G. *The War of the Worlds.* London: Heinemann, 1898.

FILMS (FICTION)

The Angry Red Planet. Sino, 1960.
Director: Ib Melchior
Screenwriters: Ib Melchior and Sid Pink
Conquest of Space, Paramount, 1955.
Director: Byron Haskins
Screenwriter: James O'Hanlon
Five Million Years to Earth. Hammer, 1967.
Director: Roy Ward Baker
Screenwriters: James Fritzell and Everett Greenbaum
Invaders from Mars. National Pictures, 1953 (remade Cannon, 1986).
Director 1953: William Cameron Menzies
Screenwriter 1953: Richard Blake
Director 1986: Tobe Hooper
Screenwriter 1986: Dan O'Bannon
Rocketship X-M. Lippert, 1950.
Director and Screenwriter: Kurt Neumann
Robinson Crusoe on Mars. Schenck-Zabel, 1964.
Director: Byron Haskins
Screenwriters: Ib Melchior and John C. Higgins
War of the Worlds. Paramount, 1953.
Director: Byron Haskins
Screenwriter: Barre Lyndon

Index

Ahrens, Thomas J., 30
Alvarez, Luis, 59
Alvarez, Walter, 59
Amino acids, 64
Ancient face of Mars, 19–21
Anderson, Poul, 101, 102
Antarctica, Earth, 30, 31, 34, 47–48, 49, 69, 70, 94
Argon, 114
Arizona State University, 40, 47
Asteroids, 19, 20, 30–31, 35, 59–60, 71, 79–80
Atmosphere, 12, 13, 21–22, 60–61, 114
Atmospheric pressure, 40–41, 54, 113
Automated probes, 29
Axis of rotation, 51

Baross, John, 66
Base, on Mars, 94–95
Biological experiments, 86
Bodenheimer, Peter, 58

Bonneville Salt Flats, 44
Brown University, 34

Caldera, 26, 27, 119
California Institute of Technology, 30
Canali, 13, 119
Canals, 13–16, 19
  deathblow to, 19
Canyons, 24, 28, 29, 40, 47
Carbon, 70
Carbon dioxide, 19, 24, 25, 54, 57, 114
Carr, Michael H., 40, 42, 43, 68
Carr, Robert H., 30
Caverns, 39
Caves, 48
Central Pacific Ridge, 66
Challenger, 85
Channels, 24, 25, 39, 40, 42, 43, 44
Charon, Pluto moon, 80
Chlorofluorocarbons, 65

Climate, 49, 50–61
    ancient atmosphere,
       60–61
    evolution of, 56–58
    weather, 54–56
Color, of Mars, 11
Cordell, Bruce, 48–49, 67
Core, 37–38
Cornell University, 49, 54
Craters, 19–21, 76, 77, 78
Crust, 31–36

Day, 12, 113
Deamer, David, 68–69
Deimos, moon, 72, 74–80,
    94, 115
    discovery, 74
    orbit, 74–75
Desert Research Institute, 68
Desert terrain, U.S., 24, 25
Dimensions, 114
Dinosaurs, 60
Discoveries, 11–13
DNA, 64, 69, 70
Dust, 18–19, 51, 78
Dust storms, 21–22, 55–56,
    58–59, 60

Earth, 12, 13, 20–21, 25–26,
    31–32, 47, 113
Earth-Moon pair, 80
Equator, 34
Escape velocity, 113, 115
Escarpment, 35–36

Fanale, Fraser P., 81–82
Fictional Mars, 96–112, 121
    at war with Mars,
       99–101
    frontier world, 105–107

humans and Martians,
    101–103
living Mars, 109–112
movies, 107–109, 122
planet of adventure,
    97–99
primitive Mars, 103–105
Films, 107–111, 122
Floods, 38, 40, 44–46, 47
Fossils, 34, 70–71
Fractures, in crust, 28
French Space Agency
    balloon, 85
Frost, 41

Galileo, 73
Ganymede, Jupiter moon,
    79–80
Gault, Donald E., 76
Geology, of Mars, 23–38
Geothermal energy, 66, 67
Glaciers, 47
Grand Canyon, Earth, 28
Gravitational field, 30
Gravity, 12–13
Great Rift Valley, Earth, 28
Great Salt Lake, Earth, 44
Greeley, Ronald, 40
Greenhouse effect, 53–54,
    57, 119
Greg, Percy, 96
Gullies, 42

Hall, Asaph, 13, 74
Hall, crater, 77
Heinlein, Robert A., 102
Hellas Basin, 20, 54, 75
Hematite, 29
Herschel, William, 12
Hodges, Carol Ann, 36

Hot-water vents, 66, 67
Huygens, Christian, 12
Hydrogen peroxide, 65

Ice caps, 2, 34, 35
Ice, power of, 46–48
Iceland, Earth, 36
Infrared radiation, 60
Interior, 37
Internal heat, 37, 58
Iron, 37
Iron oxide, 29

Jet Propulsion Laboratory
  (JPL), 40, 44, 51
Jupiter, 37, 58, 73, 79

Kasting, James F., 57, 58, 60,
  61
Kepler, Johannes, 73, 74
Kerridge, John F., 71
Keynes, Milton, 30
Kornbluth, C. M., 101
Kline, Otis Adelbert, 98
Krakatoa, Earth volcano,
  60

Lewis, C. S., 97
Lake Bonneville, 44
Lake Missoula, Earth, 46
Lander, 86–87
LaPalma Observatory, 75
Lava, 24, 27, 32, 36, 39, 40
Lick Observatory of Santa
  Cruz, 58
Life, 12–13, 61, 62–71
  fossils, 70–71
  intelligent, 13–14
Lifeless world, 18–19
Lowell Observatory, 14

Lowell, Percival, 14–16, 18,
  95, 97
Lucchitta, Baerbel, 46–47
Lure of Mars, 83–95

MacColl, Hugh, 96
Magma, 31–32, 33, 37, 39,
  119
Magnetic field, 37
Malin, Michael, 47
Mariner mission, 191, 21–24,
  26–27, 51, 76, 116, 117
Mars Observer, 83–86, 118
Mars-sample return mission,
  86–87, 88
Mars mission, 23, 37, 38, 116,
  117
Martian grand canyon, 29
Martian South, 51
Mauna Loa, 26, 27–28
Maunder, E. Walter, 17, 19
Mean surface temperature,
  113
Mercury, 80
Meteorite, 30, 35
Meteorite craters, 24
  permafrost, 49
Miller, P. Schuyler, 102
Mir, space station, 90
Missions to Mars, 116–118
Moles, burrowing devices,
  86
Moon, Earth, 26, 37, 80, 115
Moon rocks, 28–29, 30
Moons, of Mars, 13, 72–82,
  113
Moore, Henry J., 36
Morris, Elliot, 36
Mountains, 32
Mullen, George H., 54

Names, of Mars, 11
NASA, 19, 22, 23, 57, 62, 71,
  83, 85–87, 89–90, 101,
  109
Neon, 30
Neptune, 37
Nickel, 37
Nitrogen, 30, 114
Niven, Larry, 101
Nix Olympica (the Snows of
  Olympus), 26
North Pole, Earth, 34
Northern hemisphere,
  24–25, 40, 44, 45
Northern ice cap, 41
Nuclear summer, 59
Nuclear winter, 58–60

O'Keefe, John D., 30
Olympus Mons, volcano, 26,
  27, 33, 35–36, 54, 75
Olympus Mons's caldera, 26,
  27, 28
Open University, 30, 70
Orbital vehicle, 86
Orbits, 50, 51–52
Oxygen, 13, 114
Ozone, 65–66

Pairs, 80
Parker, Timothy, 44
Pedestal craters, 34
Permafrost, 49
Phinney, S. A., 71
Phobos, moon of Mars,
  74–82, 115
    discovery of, 74
    orbit, 74–75
Phobos 1, 80–81, 82, 118

Phobos 2, 28, 27, 77, 81–82,
  118
Photography, 17, 18
Physical characteristics, 113,
  115
Pieri, David, 39–40
Planetary motion, 73
Planet's spin, 36
Plateaus, 26
Pluto, 80
Pluto-Charon pair, 80
Polar caps, 12, 24, 25, 49
Polar migration, 34
Polar region, Earth, 34
Priest, Christopher, 100

Radiation, 92
Radioactive carbon dioxide,
  64
Radioactive elements, 37, 38
Rain, 43, 57
Reading, 96–112, 120–121
Red color, 29
Rocks, 28–31, 70, 71
Rotation, 36
Rousch, Ted L., 60–61

Sagan, Carl, 54, 59
Salvail, James R., 81–82
Salyut, research station, 91
Sandbar-like formations, 44,
  45
Sapping, 43, 47, 119
Saturn, 73
Saturn 5, 90
Schiaparelli, Giovanni, 13,
  26, 43
Schultz, Peter H., 34, 35–36
Schyrl, Anton Maria, 7

Seasons, 50, 51–53
Seismometers, 37–38
Shield volcanoes, 27–28, 36, 119
Sinclair, Anthony, 75
Size, 12, 16–17, 58
Sky, 50, 51
Slippage, Martian crust, 35
Soil, 28–31, 38, 62–64, 86–87
Solar flares, 92
Solar heat, 51
Solar radiation, 41
South Polar cap, 19, 55
South Pole, Earth, 34
South Pole, of Phobos, 77
Southern hemisphere, 24, 25, 43, 47, 48, 53
Southern ice cap, 55
Soviet Union, 22, 23, 28, 29, 37, 38, 80–81, 82, 83, 85, 86–87
Space station, 89–90
Spokane floods, Earth, 46
Squyres, Stephen W., 49
Stickney, Phobos crater, 77, 78
Storms, 50
Sun, 13, 56, 65, 66
Surface, 24–28, 56, 64–66
    area, 83
    beneath it, 31–33
    gravity, 113
    temperatures, 68
Surface lines, 13, 16
Surface temperatures, 50
Surface rover, 86–87

Tanaka, Kenneth, 36

Tectonic plates, 31–32, 33, 34, 119
Telescopes, 11–12, 23–24, 73
Temperature, 18, 41, 51, 53, 54, 113
Terrestrial desert, 42, 43
Terrestrial organisms, 68, 71
Tharsis Bulge, plateau, 26, 28, 36
Thermal measurement, of temperature, 18
Thorium, 37, 38
Titan, Saturn moon, 80
Titan 3 rocket, 85
Triton, Neptune moon, 80

Ultraviolet radiation, 65
Underground life, 66–67
United States Geological Survey (USGS), 36, 40, 46, 60
University of Arizona, 71
University of California, 59, 68–69, 71
University of Hawaii, 81
Uranium, 37, 38
Uranus, 2
United States, 86–95, 116–118
U.S. Naval Observatory, 13
U.S.S.R., 86–95, 116–118
USGS, 40, 46, 68

Valles Marineris, canyon, 28, 29, 36, 43–44
Vegetation, 18
Venus, 26, 37, 71
Vesta, 85–86, 118

Viking mission, 22, 23, 28, 30, 34, 37, 38, 42, 43, 50, 60, 62–64, 71, 76, 117–118
Von Braun, Wernher, 89

Water, 13–16, 19, 38, 39–49, 54, 57, 79, 81, 94, 114
  a scarce commodity, 40–41
  argument for water, 41–43
  largest known supply, 25
  more evidence, 43–44
  power of ice, 46–48
  power of water, 44–46
  search for, 48–49
Wedekind, John A., 76
Weightlessness, 91–92
Wells, H. G., 99
Wharton, Robert, 68
Wilkes subglacier, Earth, 47
Wind, 50, 55
Winter, 51
Wright, Ian P., 70–71

Year, 113
Yellowstone National Park, 66

Zond 2, 116